ELFRIDA NEXT DOOR

A NOVEL

Susan Barrett

Copyright © 2020 Susan Barrett

First published by Pencross Books

July 2020

ELFRIDA NEXT DOOR

a light, dark tale of mystery and suspense

by Susan Barrett

*Millie & Mike
with love, Susie*

SUSAN BARRETT

For Peter my faithful reader over 60 years

PART ONE

ANGELA 1

Angela runs her knuckles over the place in the wall where the rock is exposed. Already she feels the relief the pain brings, even though she hasn't yet drawn blood. She will continue until her knuckles are raw and bleeding. Afterwards, she will sleep. She usually does. She will not go mad.

RACHEL 1

"I'm your next door neighbour."

The words broke the silence with a violence that made Rachel jump down from the chair she was standing on. Up to that moment, she'd had only her own thoughts for company. Not even the fellowship of a radio. That was in one of the boxes still to be unpacked.

"Oh, I'm sorry. I didn't mean to startle you."

Rachel grabbed the back rail of the chair to steady herself, then pushed her hair out of her eyes to see more clearly the figure silhouetted in the kitchen doorway. A cap. Gumboots. Next door neighbour. She was immediately on the alert. This man would be important to her, for good or bad.

"Name's Nicolas Clarkson."

Rachel was about to respond with her own name but he was continuing to speak. "Going up or coming down?" He pointed to the curtain pole that was hanging at an angle, still attached to one of its wall brackets. "Can I help?"

His voice held the hint of an accent she thought of as Celtic, never being able to distinguish between Scottish and Irish, in fact anything other than southern English.

"Well, it was coming down and then I thought I'd better keep it. I do have a pair of curtains with rings sewn on that will do for the time being but now it's stuck." Not having spoken to anyone but the removal men since leaving London three days ago, she was conscious of blathering on like an idiot.

"So you want to keep it?"

He sounded surprised.

"For the moment, at any rate." He was right; it was a mistake to keep any of the old things left behind in the house. They'd only make her think of the elderly couple who had died there, one after the other, with only a month between them; or so the agent had told her. She didn't want ghosts.

The black curtain pole with its pair of wrought iron brackets was typical of the many things she had to decide about. The kitchen dresser presented the biggest dilemma. It was covered in black, treacly varnish. Her immediate concern, however, was the man in the doorway, her next door neighbour. Did she want to be beholden to him before she had time to get a sense of what he was like? Oliver had warned her. Be circumspect, he'd told her. This is what she had to be for at least the first six months. She'd never last that long. She'd make good friends fast. She and her brother were not alike. He knew nobody around here, at least nobody to speak of, yet he'd been weekending not far away from this Devonshire valley for years. She was going to live here permanently. She'd need helpful neighbours.

"Thank you, that would be marvellous," she said with a smile. When he didn't move, she added, "Don't worry about your boots. As you can see, we're knee-deep in dirt." She heard herself gabbling. Why had she said "we" when the whole point of being here was to live completely on her own?

Her neighbour made no move to help with the curtain pole. He was looking around the room. "The Johnsons were elderly.," he said.

Rachel was about to respond but the pause was not long enough. He was continuing. "They weren't managing. The garden. The house. Mr Johnson was the last one to die. Over two years ago. Complications with the will."

"I think I was lucky that the sale went through so easily when it came on the market."

"Yes."

Rachel waited for more but she already suspected that conversations with her neighbour would not have an easy two-way flow. He stood silently, blocking the doorway. Was he one of those people who offer help and do nothing? Or did he have some disability? Would she need to make allowances for him in some way? She shifted the position of the chair she'd been standing on.

"I came over because I need to instruct you in our parking rules." He spoke with sudden urgency.

"Oh."

"If you can spare a minute."

"Oh, certainly," she replied, reassured by the added courtesy.

He stood back as though to let her pass. "Out there?" she asked.

"Where else? This is about *parking*."

Now he sounded like an irritated schoolmaster. She must go cautiously. She wouldn't do her usual thing of summing people up at the drop of a hat.

He waited on the path while she shuffled into her galoshes. She was pleased with these rubber, backless overshoes. She'd bought them especially for her new life style and she'd keep them always ready, beneath the bench in the front porch. A tangle of honeysuckle and clematis all but made a cave of the porch. Her excitement at the move rose again as she followed Nicolas down the path. He was beating back the nettles and brambles on either side with his stick.

"I'll deal with this when I've got straight indoors," she said.

"That would be a shame."

A shame?

He turned his head towards her and spoke emphatically. "I like to encourage the wildlife."

Rachel would describe this encounter for Oliver's entertainment. *I could imagine tigers peering out of the bushes*, she'd say.

Her neighbour strode on ahead, using his stick like a conductor's baton to point up his words. *Butterflies. Eggs. Long grass.* Rachel could only catch the occasional word flung over his shoulder. She was trying to gauge her response to this man but having difficulty. She wasn't certain whether to be nervous of him or amused by him.

"Towards the end, the Johnsons didn't have a car but they did have visitors and that caused a problem."

Oh dear. Would she cause a problem? Parking etiquette? What could that mean? They had now reached the parking space, a large rectangle of gravelled ground at the head of the entrance track that led from the lane. As she'd understood from the agent, it was shared between the two properties: her cottage and her neighbour's house were both hidden behind a high evergreen hedge. This hedge enclosed the parking space on three sides, with archways cut in the high green wall on opposite sides giving access to the paths leading to each house. There looked to be plenty of room for a number of cars. Two removal lorries had parked here, as well as her own Nissan. Perhaps that was the problem. Maybe her neighbour, who'd been away while she moved in, had come back early and found he couldn't park close to his house. He'd have had to go back to the barn where he kept his car. Not really a bother, but it had been raining that day.

Nicolas was now drawing her attention with his stick to the house names painted on boards stuck into the ground below the evergreen hedge*: Priory Cottage* in gothic script, barely legible under creeping ivy, with an arrow pointing left; and *Torridon* in large, black letters, with an arrow pointing right.

"The boards are placed at the exact centre, you can bring a measure if you like."

She was amazed. She'd do no such thing. What an extraordinary thing to say.

"The area from the midway point between the signs marks the boundary between our two properties. You to the left, coming in from the lane. Torridon to the right."

She was interested in the use of 'you' for the cottage, while he referred to his house by its name. Was this significant in any way? She realised that all her senses were alert, as though she were in danger. His stick, she noticed, was topped by a section of an antler. His thumb moved restlessly in the crook of it. She began to entertain the notion that her neighbour was disturbed in some abstrusely psychological way.

"I did forewarn your husband of the difficulties."

"Husband? I'm not married!" How quickly she'd put him straight on that! She wanted to be known as a single woman in her new neighbourhood.

"But I saw --- who was the man that looked at the cottage in May?"

"My brother."

"Not married then." It sounded as though this was just a memo to himself rather than a comment to be shared.

"No." She said the word firmly

She watched as he drew a line with his stick in the gravel. He started from the midway point between the signs and continued towards the entrance track. She very much hoped that her unmarried status wouldn't lead him to think she was fair game. She vowed to be watchful. The agent had described Nicolas Clarkson as a single man, but one who had been married in the past. A widow or divorced. No children.

The way he was poking at the gravel, every so often redoing a section to correct its trajectory, unsettled her. It took a while before he was satisfied. Then he straightened and moved towards her.

"I know you will be aware of this line even if it doesn't remain clear in reality. Your little car is at present on the wrong side of the line."

"I'll move it right now. Just wait while I get the key."

She was surprised to sound so meek and placatory. Not her usual self at all. After this, the line was engraved in her memory if not permanently visible in the gravel. It was tested the next Saturday when Oliver visited.

"Oh god! The line! The line!" she cried, pushing past him the moment he arrived on her doorstep. She didn't give him time to ask what she meant but ran down the path to the car park. There was her blue Nissan Micra tucked neatly in the corner nearest the entrance track. Oliver's sports car was parked bang in the middle with its nose in Priory Cottage's territory but its rear in Torridon's. She went rushing back. "You must move your car!"

"Why on earth?" He was in the kitchen, filling the kettle with water.

She explained about the line.

Oliver switched the kettle on. "There's oceans of room. In any case he's out."

"How do you know?"

"His car's not there." His tone was pitying. "Where do you keep tea bags?"

"But did you look in the field by the gate? He keeps his car in a barn. Did you notice?"

"Why the alarm? Tea bags? Mug or teapot?"

"You haven't met him."

"I have. First time here, when I was prospecting for you. Way back in May. He seemed a perfectly decent bloke. He can't be worried by a visitor. I won't be long in any case. Where are the mugs? Builders? Earl Grey?"

Rachel grabbed his sleeve and attempted to lead him back to the parking. "Please move it. You must! He made it clear. He drew a line down the middle."

"Drew a line? Good lord."

"Well, just with his stick in the gravel. It's rained since then. The line hardly shows. But I know what he wants. Strict halves, lengthways."

Oliver complied reluctantly but when he returned to the kitchen he made it clear that he thought her agitation unwarranted. He would excuse her state, he said, because of what she'd been through recently.

That sent her temperature up. "State! What do you mean? I'm not in a state. I'm fine."

Oliver raised one of his eyebrows, something he'd practised for days as a boy. His quizzical expression usually appeased her but she was too upset by the way he wasn't taking her anxiety seriously. Perhaps it would have been better if he'd left the car parked any old how in the middle of the space. Nicolas Clarkson would have come to complain. Then Oliver would have been able to see what he was like. Her nerves still jangling, she took over the tea-making. Oliver sat down at the table and watched as she put two tea bags in the pot. Before the kettle boiled, she added two more. Finally, she took one out.

She knew Oliver was watching her. "Stop it," she said. "You're making me feel like a contestant in a cookery programme."

Oliver smiled.

"Okay. I am a bit harried. But there's something about my neighbour that I find unsettling. For instance –" She hesitated as she struggled to find something about Clarkson that would convince Oliver of his oddness. Nothing came immediately to mind. Maybe she wasn't being fair; after all, she'd barely met the man. She admitted she was in a heightened state of anxiety, due to leaving London and her job with such haste, and in such a turmoil of emotion. She'd probably misjudged Clarkson. He had every right to be careful about the boundaries between the two properties. She just wasn't used to having a close neighbour in this countrified way: right on top of her in the middle of nowhere, just acres and acres of green fields and trees. She'd get to know him. She'd have time to cook proper meals now, and she could invite him over. He was probably lonely. She'd invite Oliver, too, just to be safe. Nicolas might be very much older than she was, but in her experience age difference didn't preclude any man from thinking she'd welcome an advance.

"He offered to help fix the curtain rail. I'd got it half down."

"Well, that was a neighbourly offer."

"Yes, but then instead of helping, he dragged me outside to show me the boundaries."

"Ah. Good. Is there a fence between the gardens? When I first visited I couldn't make out where one garden began and the other ended, not just at the front but at the back too."

"There are fences but they're mostly broken."

Oliver was playing with his mug, moving it to and fro between the shelter of each hand. Rachel knew he doubted whether her solicitor had done a good enough job on her behalf. Although younger by two years, he always checked up on her business transactions. He didn't even trust her agent to make sure her fees were high enough, even though he had no experience whatsoever in the world of children's book illustration. Now he was offering to check all the papers regarding the sale, something she hadn't really bothered to do in any depth.

"I left it all to the solicitor," she said. "I'm sure he did a good job, checking everything."

"So who, for instance, does the priory belong to?"

Rachel felt a sudden jolt. Forgetting something important was a recurring nightmare. "The priory?" It was as though she'd never heard the word before.

"Ruins of."

Was Oliver's eyebrow about to go up again?

"Oh yes. The priory ruins." Yes, she had seen them marked on the map but she was sure they didn't lie on her land. They lay at the bottom of Torridon's garden.

"Did he cover you for chancel repair liability?"

She had no idea what he was referring to. That fazed her for a second but she could see the map clearly in her head. A blue line defined Priory Cottage and its garden, with the house in the north east corner taking up about a fifth of the land, while the neighbouring property was delineated in red, with the house lying in a similar position but in a larger area of garden. The jagged line between the two properties made them look like the corners of a jigsaw, slotted together with no intervening pieces. They formed a square in the midst of fields belonging to Priory Farm. The track leading across one of the fields from the council lane was outlined in both blue and red. All this Rachel could see clearly in her illustrator's mind's eye. She was less sure of the word Barn in italic script beside a small shape just before the track joined the parking space. The faint shape had no colour outline. Nicolas had appropriated an old barn as his garage. She was not worried at the absence of a garage on her own property. Nor was she worried by this ominous mention of some kind of liability. The ruins of the priory were marked at the end of Clarkson's property furthest from his house. She could depend on her visual memory. "If there's any liability to do with the priory it's nothing to do with me," she said with conviction. "I'll let you have the box file of photocopies of all the papers. You're welcome to check."

Later she went with him as he left. Nicholas Clarkson was about to pass through the Torridon archway in the evergreen hedge as they emerged through theirs. All three hesitated as they regarded each other. It looked to Rachel as though Clarkson was about to turn away but Oliver had already called out and was crossing towards him. The two men met out of earshot. She was reluctant to join them. It seemed to her that her neighbour didn't want to be neighbourly. Wishing Oliver hadn't decided to strike up a conversation, she raised a hand in distant greeting as she made her way slowly to his neatly parked car. Clarkson could have no cause for complaint.

Oliver joined her after a minute or two.

"Well?" she asked." "What did he say?"

"Nothing very much. Just pleasantries. He seems a perfectly normal sort of bloke to me. Except ..." He broke off. "Are you going to be on gate-duty for me?"

The gates, one at each end of the track, had been a topic for discussion between them when Rachel was about to put in an offer on the cottage. Oliver thought she would find it a pain to keep opening and shutting the gates as she drove in and out. There were cows grazing in the field the track crossed. She wouldn't be able to leave the gates open, even when the cows weren't in the field. Any stock being driven down the lane would take the opportunity to peel off from the herd and lumber in to graze fresh grass. She bowed to her brother's greater experience but didn't let what they called gate duty put her off from buying the cottage she'd fallen for.

She opened the first gate and gave Oliver an exaggerated bow as he drove through. He leant across to open the passenger door for her. "Except," he said again as she got in. "When I expressed interest in looking at the boundaries ..." Oliver spoke slowly as he negotiated the hummocks and holes in the red-earth and stony track, before resuming. "As soon as I mentioned boundaries, he broke off the conversation and rushed away as though his house was in flames."

"Yes. I know. Stop-start-stop – that's what I've found, too. He's chatting away quite sensibly, and then suddenly he's off. It's as though you've committed some dreadful misdemeanour, without any clue as to what it was."

"You could allow him his parking phobia."

"But drawing a line in the gravel! He could have just said something."

"But he's clearly harmless, even if he is slightly odd."

"All the same, I'll go carefully. You should be pleased." Rachel got out to open the further gate onto the lane. Oliver unwound his window and she leant in to brush his cheek with her mouth. She checked he had the box file of papers on the back seat and he promised to go through them when he had the chance. It was good to have her brother within easy visiting distance.

She stood in the lane, waving at the departing car. As she closed the gate and started walking back to the cottage, she was surprised by a twinge of fear in the pit of her stomach. There was no-one else she could call on in emergency, and he was always busy, pushing and pulling his patients' skeletons into place.

Her feet moved as though they belonged to someone else: brashly white, brand new trainers, placed one in front of the other, avoiding the deeper ruts. How had this happened? How did she come to be walking home, down a field track rather than a city pavement? The move from London to Devon seemed an act carried out not by her but by someone she only vaguely knew. Her mind went back several months.

She'd acted in a fit of temper. Yes, but temper was nothing new. She'd raged at Malcolm many times over their years together. Each time, he'd made up for whatever it was that had caused her anger. She'd returned to loving him for what he was: a lover and friend whose first loyalty was not to her. There was nothing upsetting about that. It was her choice. It suited her to live on her own. She valued her independence, even though in her logical mind she knew she wasn't independent at all. She was dependent on Malcolm for work and for love. Without him, she'd be nothing. That's what she'd half-believed; it was certainly what she used to tell him, a sop to his ego at a cost to her own. Now it was time to remember exactly who she was; the person she'd come into the world to be.

Sally, fellow artist and similarly single, had been warning her for years. All very well to fall for him in the first place. After all, he was her publisher. Rachel was fairly confident he would have taken her on as writer and illustrator, even if they hadn't gone back to her flat after their first meeting at a book launch party. The first in the Walter the Wicked Warthog series had come out ten years ago. Sally had been thrilled to see Rachel so happy. That was before Rachel had discovered that Malcolm's wife was still present in his life. He hadn't left her at all. To her subsequent shame, she'd accepted all his arguments in favour of their arrangement until one March day. Malcolm had done what he'd done many times in the past: not followed through on a promise of a weekend together. He'd rung on the Friday. He couldn't get out of attending an end of term concert in which one of his children was playing a part. He was so very sorry. He'd make it up to her the following Wednesday when he could stay overnight. He'd pick up food and wine and see to the meal. As he talked, she could see the scene. He'd light candles and tell her to put her feet up until the food was ready. Who could possibly complain?

She could.

It was as though a hurricane had picked her up, hurled her into the air, and destroyed everything in her wake. Anger had seen her through all her decisions. Now she was walking towards her new home. It could be the worst mistake of her life. Having spent years accepting a poor situation, she had erupted in a fury that swept her to the further extreme. She'd given up everything: career, lover, London life.

In a more rational state, she could have simply broken with Malcolm. She could have - perhaps? – found another publisher and moved to a cheaper part of London. But caution had stepped in. Sales were decreasing. Her style of illustration was outdated. She disliked using computer software which produced cruder images than she aimed for. If she worked at it, people said, she'd succeed, they were sure. But Rachel wasn't willing to try. The prospect of a gentler life in the country, as put forward by her brother, appealed to her. Oliver had drawn closer to her now their parents had died. *Orphans in the storm*, he said to her. His partner Matt had turned out to be a married man and Oliver was doing his best to adjust to the way Matt now only saw him occasionally, whereas he had been live-in for more than a year. *Matt and Malcolm, both heels*, said Oliver.

Nice men do exist, thought Rachel as she drew near the gate to the car park, even if they are few and far between. She might find one. Oliver would introduce her to his Exeter friends. There would be new things to learn about. She would start sketching again, in watercolours and pencil. Oliver said there were lots of opportunities to show her work. Her spirits rose as she looked up to take in the view.

It was the tail end of an August day and long shadows lay across the field from the hedgerow trees. Their leaves were already tinged russet, through a summer's lack of rain. The distant hills that enclosed the valley were wooded. She named the colours she would choose to paint them. The box of materials was still to be unpacked in the room she'd chosen as a studio: the larger bedroom with a window in the eaves. It overlooked the section of garden to the front of the house and the corner where she would always park the Nissan. It was a view not interesting enough to draw her attention away from work. Yes, she would get unpacked and settled.

Sally would be pleased at her swift change of mood. Attitude is everything was one of Sally's mantras. A situation may be dire and not of your making, but it's your response to it you can control.

Rachel was at the gateway when she realised, with a twinge of foreboding, she'd left the gate open. She'd got into Oliver's car, knowing she'd be back in a couple of minutes. It wouldn't be worth shutting the gate. Clarkson hadn't been around to notice the misdemeanour.

She was wrong.

"Hoy!"

The voice startled her. It was Clarkson. He emerged from the dark interior of the barn and joined her as she was about to shut the gate. He placed a hand on the rail, not far from her own.

"You clearly weren't aware of the danger," he said.

Danger? What did he mean?

"The cows." He pointed towards a rise in the field. "Even if you can't see them." The field looked empty. "They may not be in the field today. You can't risk it. Always shut the gate behind you, even if it's just for a few minutes."

The worst part of this, Rachel thought when she was back in the cottage, was the realisation that Clarkson had been watching her from inside his garage. He might look like a nice man: even features, broad forehead, wavy, grey hair. But he made her nervous.

ANGELA 2

Nicolas has brought me a tin box. He says it was used to keep ammunition dry during the first world war. My stock of bright yellow A4 paper was getting too damp to use. This strikes me as appropriate. Not that what I write can be seen as ammunition. It will never be used, its only purpose being to keep me sane. Writing things down helps. It's good to get my thoughts out, down, onto paper; Marilou told me that. Otherwise they buzz about my head like so many angry hornets. They could send me mad. I will not go mad.

You might find it surprising that Nicolas supplies me with paper and allows me to write. That's easy to explain. He acquired reams of recycled paper, part of an auction lot of office equipment. So it doesn't cost him a thing. Also, he has no curiosity at all in me or my inner life; he never did have. He is not in the least interested in what I'm writing. He couldn't care less now that he has me exactly where he wants me: completely under his thumb. I can squiggle and squirm. A lot of good would that do me. I'm invisible, to all intents and purposes. I always was.

But now I am putting myself on paper. The written sheets go back into the box. Slowly, the pile will grow, and I will exist. Here I go.

My name is Angela. I was married to Nicolas for … but often, at this point, I get confused. Time has lost all meaning. I've lost all meaning. What is it to be alive, and yet not live?

I tug at my chaotic thoughts to bring them back to the simple mathematics of time. I was born in a rectory. The fact stabilises me. But how long have I been married? My mind goes foggy. Perhaps if I could really focus, I'd remember all the facts in my life and forget the feelings. This is the exercise I at least attempt on a regular basis.

I was a clever child, I'm sure of that. My best school friend was called Denise. She had two, long, thick, chestnut-coloured plaits which lay neatly and evenly down her back, nearly reaching her waist and her grey regulation skirt. My hair was thin. It grew in pathetically limp strands which never got beyond the base of my neck before needing to be cut. My father said it was 'time for pruning'. He thought hair was like the wisteria over the veranda. A good prune and it would flower well next year. My hair never did grow well. Did I, Angela, ever flower? I doubt it. My father called me his angel. So did Nicolas in our early days. I was obedient and therefore acceptable.

RACHEL 2

The village hall throbbed with the excitement of the Saturday market. Stalls ran the length of the room, leaving a narrow passageway between the two lines and the central block. Women, children and the occasional stray man moved slowly around the room. Everyone seemed to be talking to everyone else. Rachel hesitated in the doorway as though on a riverbank. She could either enter and become a member of this community – something which would surely follow her first interaction – or she could remain a visitor, never taking part. She guessed her choice was as simple as that.

She'd heard about the market from her first acquaintances in the valley: the farmer and his wife at Priory Farm. An exploratory walk around the lanes had taken her to its front door. The farmhouse, Georgian by the style of its windows and doorway, stood right on the lane.

"I know what you're thinking," said the woman who was vigorously polishing the door's brass, hand-shaped knocker. "What's a farmhouse doing without a decent bit of garden between it and passing traffic. It's like going to town without a hat. At least that's what my mother-in-law used to say and I repeat it to our B and Bs."

As Rachel had nothing to say to this, the polisher continued. "You've bought Priory Cottage, haven't you. Welcome to the valley. Come on in and have a cuppa." Rachel followed her inside, appreciating the warmth and flow of the country woman's voice. This was the kind of neighbourly meeting she'd hoped for.

Her name was Betty. Her husband was sitting at the kitchen table. "And this is Stanley." The big man heaved himself to his feet. He beamed at her. She could draw them both, round-cheeked, red-faced farmers. The room smelt faintly of stale milk. "We're one of the many Middletons round here. You'll see."

Stanley shook her hand, making it feel like a collection of bird bones.

Betty was continuing. "If you're lost for a name, just say Middleton. That'll see you right."

"She's right. Just say Middleton."

The couple had a good laugh at this. Rachel smiled. "That's easy, then," she said. "I'm called Rachel. Rachel Hines."

"Oh my goodness me. The Walter the Wicked what's it Rachel Hines? My goodness me, Stan, they were right."

The Middletons had heard from someone who'd heard from someone else that the new person at Priory Cottage was the children's book author who'd appeared on CeeBeeBees not long before. "We could scarcely believe it. Our grandchildren love Walter. They have all the Walter books. Oh, wait 'til I tell Clara. She'll be tickled pink."

Clara was their youngest daughter who lived nearby. Rachel was given details of their children, grandchildren, Betty's parents (she'd grown up far afield, which turned out to be Dorset), Stanley's family and the history of Priory Farm. "This room tisn't really the kitchen, leastways ee wasn't in olden times," said Stanley. He swivelled in his chair to jerk his thumb at the inglenook fireplace. A shining modern electric stove stood within it. "Twas whatee called the orl."

This fazed Rachel for a moment but she swiftly adjusted her understanding. It was like getting the gist of a conversation in a foreign language, without bothering about individual words. They were sitting in what had been called the hall. It originally had a central fireplace and a hole in the ceiling for the smoke but the ceiling was in fact the roof. Thatched like today and still supported by the same framework of hazel branches. The family had lived in the hall, eating and sleeping. Across the passageway had been the place for the animals with a loft above, reached by a ladder. More of the family had slept up there. Rachel wasn't sure whether to take Stanley's word for all this. Oliver would know. He'd read about local architecture.

"Of course, it's changed a lot," said Betty. "The place where the animals were kept is now our best room. Just fancy that! If we could go back in time, we'd not recognise anything round here. I expect you know there was a religious establishment here, once upon a time. We were the farm for the priory. Then Henry the Eighth came along and got rid of all the monasteries. The priory ceased to exist and the land went into private ownership. The fishponds are still there, but just as a swampy bit of ground. It's on Torridon's land, like the ruins. Have you met your next door neighbour?"

The conversation took a fresh direction and eventually led to the need, as the Middletons saw it, for Rachel to go to the Saturday market. "I'll look out for you," said Betty.

Hesitating in the doorway of the village hall, Rachel felt momentarily daunted. It was full; in fact, so full it would be hard to spot Betty. More likely, Betty would notice her first. Her height, not remarkable in London, put her head and shoulders over most of the throng. Her pony-tailed hair, blonde with the streak of Dark Tulip, probably stood out from all the greying heads. With relief, she saw Betty waving at her vigorously from a stall far down on one side.

Betty was selling garden produce. Piled high on her stall were heaps of runner beans, beetroot, earth-covered potatoes, spring onions, and onions plaited into strings. "Impressive," said Rachel. "All your own work?"

"Stan does the taters."

Rachel decided to buy a couple of beetroot but Betty wouldn't let her. "Put that away," she said, nodding to Rachel's purse at the same time as attending to another customer. She piled runner beans into handheld scales. "I'll call in on you later. Just hold on a mo. I want to introduce you to next door."

Rachel understood that Betty did not mean a Priory Farm neighbour – there were no other houses close to the farm, save for Torridon and her own cottage – but the stall holder beside her in the line. There was no-one behind the stall although it held something for sale: a small pyramid of jars against which was propped a cardboard notice. It bore a single word in red capitals: HONEY.

"Oh, he must have popped out again. Just hang on. He'll be back."

Rachel was not going to wait around. She didn't need to be introduced to anyone. She moved away with Oliver's advice in mind. "They'll want to take you over," he'd said. "Be cautious."

Rachel found her blue Nissan hemmed in by other cars in the village car park. Caution wasn't an option. For the next quarter of an hour, she welcomed a number of interactions with helpful people and eventually she was able to drive away. She resolved to follow her own instincts about people. Being cool was not her style. She had already been told to drop in "whenever you want" by two separate couples living in the centre of the village. She was going to be alright here. Moving had been a good decision. She would set up her studio and start work on her own subjects; Wicked Walter had come to the end of his natural life. She was beginning a new phase of hers.

At the T-junction where the lane from the village joined the one that led further down the valley, she paused for a second, gazing across at "her" gate that opened onto "her" entrance track. She was conscious of feeling possessive. At the same time, and maybe because of this feeling, she was aware that something had changed. Before crossing over the junction, she gazed hard at the track entrance, trying to work out what looked different.

Then she saw that a sign had been put up to the right of the gate. It announced that the track was private. Nothing wrong with that. Nicolas Clarkson might be on the strange side but she was getting used to him. Perhaps he'd had a difficult childhood; perhaps he had been made redundant or something; people often have reasons for being a pain; she was prepared to make allowances. She drove across the lane and stopped in the space before the entrance gate. The new sign was painted in big black letters on a board tacked to a post pushed into the wide grass verge. It read: PRIVATE ACCESS ONLY TORRIDON.

It was probably necessary to announce that the track was private. She liked the feeling that only people she knew and invited would drive down the track to find her. But what was it about the notice that disturbed her? She drove through the gateway, stopped the car, got out, walked back and read the notice again before shutting the gate.

Clarkson had arranged the words in four lines, one word per line.

What was his intention? Did he mean that the track only granted access, with Torridon as a kind of signature to the message? Or did he mean that access was only to Torridon. There was no room below Torridon to include Priory Cottage. He could have squeezed in Priory but that would have signalled that people could visit the ruins, and Nicolas had already made it clear to her that the ruins were not open to the public.

She went on puzzling this over, and gauging her varying responses to it, for the rest of the morning when Betty called in on her way home.

"You saw the notice?" Rachel asked as soon as she'd arrived.

Betty had seen it but she hadn't been surprised. "Typical, if you ask me," she said.

"But no mention of Priory Cottage? Actually, I felt quite angry."

"Oh well, that's no surprise. We're all left feeling angry after having anything to do with Mr Clarkson."

She filled Rachel in with descriptions of occasions when Nicolas had done or said something that badly upset different people from a whole cast of local people. Just before she left, after a long chat over the vegetables she'd piled on the kitchen table, she added one more instance of strange Clarkson behaviour.

"You may have difficulty in getting anyone to trim the hedge around the car park. The last person stormed out halfway through. He couldn't take all the fussy interference." Betty imitated Clarkson's voice. *"You've left out a bit here. Mind this, that, and the other.* He had to finish it himself with Stan's hedge-trimmer. He hated to have to ask for the loan because they fell out years ago, over the boundary hedge. He asked our grandson to help once. But our Brinley wouldn't do it. He didn't even start. Nicolas had told him that, if he didn't do it properly, he wouldn't get paid. Brinley was livid. He went, like, if he doesn't think I can do it, he shouldn't ask me in the first place. He couldn't believe Clarkson could be so churlish. We could, because we're used to the poor man."

"Poor man?"

"Yes, we have to feel sorry for him. On his own with no news."

Rachel waited for an explanation, sure that Betty wouldn't withhold gossip.

"You'll hear soon enough. His wife left him some three years ago and he hasn't heard a word from her since. We've given up asking."

ANGELA 3

I dread losing my mind. I exercise my brain by giving myself imaginary sums to do and remembering poetry learnt by heart. Sometimes, when I'm feeling strong, I recite aloud. Other times, my voice sounds too croaky for the task. It's easier to keep it all, silently, in my head. Any lapse of memory can be glided over. I stray from a silent poem into memories of schooldays. This slides into another category of mental exercise that comes under the heading Time and Place Maps. In the School Map, I move in my imagination up the steps to the convent's gothic entrance, down the stone-flagged corridor to the dining hall; up the two flights of stone stairs to the dormitories. A bell clangs. Girls in navy-blue skirts, white blouses and striped ties stream down flights of stairs in different parts of the building to crowd together towards the classroom wing. Silence! Silence! No talking! No running! Leaving a prefect issuing such orders halfway down the corridor, I wander around the block, trying to place the room where I began to come alive, thanks to the Latin teacher. Strange that a passion for a dead language brought me fully into the present. My childhood home in the rectory held no spark of life. My parents were elderly. We were always super-polite. I fell in love with Catullus.

I've asked for books but so far without success. I'll go on trying, though. I have to keep my mind sharp.

Clever clogs, Denise called me. I liked the admiring tone but was doubtful of its truth. I never wanted to be top in class. I didn't want to be better at anything than anyone else. "Do as you would be done by," was the rectory mantra. I was awarded a star for posture, and it was removed. "You have begun to slouch, Angela. Stand up straight." Since that moment, I have never stood up straight. I daresay that helps me in these close quarters.

Nowadays, my shoulders ache. It's due to the camp bed's thin, lumpy mattress. I plead for the mattress from the spare room. No luck. I have no bargaining power. No power at all.

RACHEL 3

From the kitchen window Rachel watched Oliver stumping his way down the garden, a long-handled hook over his shoulder. She smiled. Her little brother, off on an important mission. Not much different in his early 40s from the lad he'd been in his teens. When their father had his first stroke, Oliver had taken on the heavy gardening jobs, his determination greater than his strength or capabilities. Stump, stump, stump – his back view, then as now, announced his intentions. She could almost hear his thoughts: I shall beat this jungle come what may. Many of the jobs in childhood had been too much for him; for her, too, which worried their mother who was growing increasingly incapable with multiple sclerosis. It was awful to say it – neither of them ever expressed it aloud - but life became much easier when their parents died within a year of each other. She and Oliver sold up the home in Wimbledon and moved into flats. They'd stayed closely in touch until Oliver moved out of London to set up his own practice as an osteopath in Exeter. With her move to the country, encouraged by Oliver, they would be close again. This is what she hoped. His sometimes-partner, Matthew, had gone back to his wife and family. Each time this happened, Rachel was spitting mad on her brother's behalf. He was far too willing to put up with poor situations for fear of losing out altogether. Perhaps, it came to her today, she was like him in this? She'd put up with her half-relationship with Malcolm for far too long. Like Oliver, she could easily fall into depression, through a reluctance to make difficult choices.

Still, this morning, with Oliver with her for the whole day, they were both feeling cheerful. He'd brought back the box file of old papers, passed on by the Johnsons' solicitors. He would fill her in, later on, with whatever he'd learnt. First, he was set on clearing as much of the undergrowth from the fence which divided her garden from Torridon's. The previous weekend, they'd hacked away at brambles and overgrown shrubs to reveal a yard or two of shaky, wooden panelling. Now the task was to establish what would need to be done to create a clear and firm boundary between the two properties. She hoped that in the next few months they would clear the thickets of undergrowth further down the garden where the fence gave way to a high bank topped with a hedge. Once she'd got the joint in the oven – special treat, recreating childhood Sundays rarely created in the first place – she'd join Oliver. She could do with some vigorous slash and burn.

A bonfire! They used to love lighting and stoking them at the bottom of the Wimbledon garden. She hurried on with the kitchen jobs, sticking cloves of garlic and V's of rosemary into the shoulder of lamb. I'm happy, she told herself in surprise. Actually happy, for the first time for years. Not anxious, not sad, not hurried, but happy.

Garden implements had been left in a shed, each item cleaned, oiled and attached by its neck to a rail. The old couple's inheritors had not touched a thing. This meant that the garden shed was in the state it had been left – ordered and clean, while the cottage itself had been filthy and chaotic. She chose a pitch fork and a wide-pronged leaf rake and went to join Oliver, following the path he had beaten through the long grass and thistles.

Before they became too old, the Johnsons had clearly spent more time outside than inside. Underneath the thickets of hawthorn and bramble and grass uncut for years, there was evidence of circular flower beds, a maze of stone-lined paths, two long herbaceous borders. The hints of a garden plan and careful planting spurred Rachel on. She would restore it. First, it was a matter of finding out where her garden ended and Torridon's began.

Oliver straightened as she approached. He'd revealed a short section of fence. "Have a look. Totally rotten."

"I can replace it. Can't I? Is fencing horribly expensive?" Gazing at the sagging fence panel brought to light by Oliver's hook, she experienced a quiver of misgiving. Allowing for the sums needed to make the cottage comfortable, she'd reached the limit of her budget after buying it in the first place. She knew she'd been over optimistic about getting commissions. Her hopes had been inflated by her urgent need to get away from her London life. She sought reassurance in Oliver's expression.

"Not a problem," he said. "We can soon sort this."

"Music to my ears," she replied, beginning to scrape together the piles of vegetation in his wake. "I thought we could have a bonfire," she said.

"Sounds good."

The fire hadn't been going long – the inconsistency of the breeze worked against it – when she heard her neighbour's voice. "Hoy! Ahoy there."

His head and shoulders appeared. Rachel thought: *What now?* She felt her good mood seep out of her.

Later, over lunch, they went over Clarkson's contribution to their morning. Oliver was surprised that Rachel had taken his intervention so amiss.

"He was just being friendly. He was smiling when he approached."

"Was that a smile? More like a snarl."

"You're unfair to him. What's he done to you?"

Nothing in particular, that was true. But she had taken against the man from the moment he drew the line in the gravel. "Shouting *hoy* to get our attention is not exactly charismatic."

"I thought he was saying 'Ahoy!' in a friendly, amusing kind of way. I think he's one of those men who like to "josh", their brand of teasing. And teasing is another form of flirting. Being friendly to the opposite sex."

"He didn't strike me as being either friendly or amusing. Polluting the environment!"

"Oh, I don't think he was saying that at all. He was on about the direction of the wind."

"I distinctly heard him say that smoke from a bonfire is as polluting as the exhaust fumes from seven cars. Was it seven? Or seventy?"

"But he admitted he has bonfires himself sometimes."

"I didn't hear that. He directed all his attention at you."

"Jealous then?"

"Of course not!"

"He's quite good looking."

"Not my type."

"Nor mine."

"I'm not on the look-out for anyone. I need a total rest from any kind of involvement."

"So do I."

"Okay then. "

Still disgruntled with each other, they lapsed into silence as they ate the lamb. Then Oliver told Rachel that this was the most delicious meat he'd had in years.

"It's probably the first *meat* you've had in years."

"You're right. I do feel on holiday."

"I know what you mean."

"Nothing is either good or bad but thinking makes it so. Or words to that effect."

"Absolutely."

If only I could find a man like Oliver, Rachel thought as she carved two more slices of lamb.

After they'd cleared the kitchen table and set themselves up with coffee, Oliver produced the box file of papers. "Some brilliant old deeds," he said. "Look at this writing! Copperplate. Imagine the time it took. And maps. And a folder put together by someone who used to live here in the 19th century."

Poring over the documents, Rachel began to understand

the history and lay-out of her surroundings. The cottage had been built in the sixteenth-century, after the Priory had been abandoned following Henry VIII's dissolution of the monasteries. Priory Farm had taken over all the land ringed by the lane from the village: 80 acres of pasture, orchards, woods, fishponds and stream. The cottage had been tied to the farm, providing accommodation for an agricultural labourer and his family, but went into private ownership after the first world war.

"And what about Torridon? When did that get built?"

"In 1878, on land sold by the farmer to a retired vicar. Three acres, or four including the priory ruins. I want to ask Nicolas if I can see the ruins."

"I asked him early on, and he went all funny. But maybe he has something against me. Try it! He might like to show you around. "

"Why shouldn't he? I'd like to see *inside* Torridon, too. It has an important stained-glass window on the stairs, something to do with Art Deco, there's correspondence about that in here." He had the folder open in front of him and was riffling through the papers. "The Reverend was no impoverished churchman. His mother came from a Cornish china clay family, as far as I can make out. Hold on a moment, I want to find - yes, here we are. The Rev was a medievalist. He spent his time digging about in dusty archives, putting into modern or rather Victorian English medieval ballads. Ah here we are. This is what I really want to share with you. I'm going to read you a medieval ballad."

Oliver settled back in his chair. As a schoolboy he'd loved acting. His triumph had been as Portia in the Merchant of Venice. "Here we go. *Elfrida.* Isn't that a great name. Imagine Elfrida here, now." With his hands, he drew around his face a whimple and composed his features into a picture of demure maidenhood which made Rachel laugh. "Now listen," he admonished. "Seriously." But he hardly seemed serious when he began reciting in a mock-Victorian manner with a Robbie Burns lilt.

Elfrida was a maid so pure
No lily bloomed with such allure.
Treasured as the richest prize
E'er born beneath the kingdom's skies.

Not yet fourteen summers old,
So goes the story I was told,
She was betrothed to a Christian knight
Whose castle lay within eagle's sight.

T'would be a boon to have his daughter's swain
Lord of the land near his own domain.
Thus planned Elfrida's sire
Ensconced beside his winter's fire.

Where is he whom I'm to wed?
Such questions thronged Elfrida's head
Like swarms of bees on nectar fed.
He'll be with us soon, her mother said.

When summer's warmth melts winter's cold,
He will return with soldiers bold.
Take heed and sew your sampler bright,
Humble bride of handsome knight.

Your snow-white hand is to be gi'en
To the noble knight, when - duly shriven
Of the deaths of heathens he has killed -
The will of God will be fulfilled.

Home from the Holy Land he came

To wed Elfrida, heart aflame.
In attendance, from his bouts,
A band of ruffians, drunkards, louts.

They revelled long into the night
With riotous song and drunken fight.
Now – and woe it is to relate –
The moon beheld the maiden's fate.

Into Elfrida's chamber broke a knave
No honour, no blushes did he save
And like a boar in forest wild
He had his way, the maid defiled.

But greater than the pain or plight
Was the horror revealed by candlelight.
No vandal; just the dreadful sight
Of her betrothed, her handsome knight.

Oh woe is me, she cried but knew
Words could not hold a mirror true.
She vowed right there and then
Nevermore give time to men.

She left the home where she had dwelled
Since childhood; left the love she'd held
For kith and kin, and into the forest dark
She wound her way, her purpose stark.

The bishop of the nearest city
Heard her tale and felt much pity.
"An anchorite you can become,

And pray all day in stone-girt tomb.

Thus it was. Elfrida stepped from the living world
Into a chamber, stone-engirdled.
For four and forty years and more
Elfrida never went beyond cell door.

Yet her fame spread far and wide
Her words of wisdom were the guide
For those who bent to the narrow chink
That served as window, a worldly link.

To all, benediction did she provide,
Her trust in God she did not hide.
They say, e'en yet, her spirit does bestow
Hope and love to those below.

If on a late summer day
On forest walk you go astray,
Then you may feel the maiden pure
At your elbow, steady, sure.

She'll help restore your faith in life,
To battle on, despite the strife,
Trust in goodness, abhor the bad,
Find peace at last and be glad.

From a Collection of Medieval Ballads, transcribed in 1867 by the Reverend Eliot McElligott."

Rachel clapped her hands. "Oh, that's marvellous." She relished Oliver's enjoyment at reading aloud as much as the quaint poem itself.

"But the thing is," said Oliver. "This is about the priory. The Rev built Torridon here because he'd learnt that Elfrida had become an anchorite in this very priory!"

"What's an anchorite?"

"Someone who gives up the world, gets sealed into a cell and stays there for the rest of his or her life. I think mostly females. "

"So Elfrida -? Spent her life sealed up ...somewhere ... at the bottom of Clarkson's garden?" A chill went through her. She stretched out her hand for the poem. "I shall have to read this myself. I don't think I've quite taken it in. Is it a kind of Me-too story?"

"Yes. You could say that. And she was only 14!"

"Oh, grim, grim. I don't really want to think about that. Too close for comfort. Are you sure the Reverend got it right? Why did he think Elfrida was here, in *our* priory?"

"Read everything in the folder for yourself, then, if you don't believe me."

That night, after Oliver left, Rachel found herself listening out for the cottage's creaks and interpreting them in ways she hadn't done until now. Her mind kept circling back to the fourteen-year old girl who had decided to become a religious hermit. She'd spent the rest of her life – and how many years was that? - sealed in a cell which must still exist under the ruins just a couple of hundred yards away. Only the thinnest of veils divided medieval Elfrida in the priory from herself in the cottage now.

There was another question that persisted, making it hard to sleep.

How come the ballad written by the retired vicar, the builder of the house next door, ended up among the papers belonging to the Johnsons of Priory Cottage? Surely it belonged, in its folder of history, to the owner of Torridon?

ANGELA 4

My mind skitters around without direction. Sometimes I pretend that I'm writing about myself. By that I mean, I don't think my thoughts. I imagine writing them down. Hard to explain. It stops me getting stuck in stupidly repetitive circles, not knowing where I started and where I'm going. What is the name of the prime minister? What is the name of the prime minister? What is the name of? What is? What prime minister? Prime minister, prime minister, prime, prime, what? Yes, it gets as bad as that.

Even the trick of putting thoughts into imaginary writing doesn't really work. So, to stop myself going completely mad, I've come up with an idea. A nibby wheeze, my father used to call it. I'm going to talk to a person in my head. Not to myself, but to someone else. I shall tell this person the history of my path to my present situation. Who will it be, this person? God knows.

Wait, might my listener actually be God? That's a shivery kind of thought. I was brought up to talk to God, so maybe He'd be a good listener. At least, a listener that I'd consider a good one. God was very close to me in my childhood. No. It was Jesus who was very close to me. Gentle Jesus, meek and mild, look upon a little child. That was comforting, companionable.

Jesus can't comfort me now. Nor be a companion.

Where was I? What was I thinking? Try again. Small child, praying at her bedside in the rectory. The floor was lino. We were poor. Not like the Reverend Eliot McElligott who built Torridon.

Where to start?

How long have I been here?

Let me start when my adult life started. Let me start when I met Nicolas.

She or I?

She was just eighteen and had completed a secretarial course at the local polytechnic. Denise, her school friend, was already in Lon-

don, working as a secretary for a publishing house which specialised in medieval history and art books. Denise phoned. Leave the sticks and share our flat in Parson's Green. We're looking for a fourth. From rectory to parson's green? Like jumping from frying pan into fire? A weak joke that surprised and puzzled her new friends. They probably couldn't make her out. She was awkward. Uncertain how to "be". But somehow she managed. She got herself a job in a small printing firm. She was the receptionist, doubling as secretary to the boss, Eric Hoskins, a portly man with bad breadth and scurf. He thought she should be flattered when he laid a hand on her shoulder and kept it there just a little too long. He called her his little angel. There were younger men who took breaks from the printing presses to strut around her desk, making insinuating remarks about her to each other. How to react? She smiled and bent her head, fiddled with her pen and the appointments book.

Then one day in came someone of quite a different order. He burst into reception as though he'd been carried in on a gust of wind. She straightened.

He leant on the edge of her desk with both hands. "You'll have me down for 10," he told her. "I'm a shade early."

The r was rolled lightly. She imagined his name, Chez d'Erly. It couldn't be. She gazed down at the appointments book, finding it hard to focus on the page.

A finger tapped the right place. "Clarkson," he prompted. "Ten o'clock."

He was handsome in a conventional way. Imagine the hero as depicted on the cover of a romantic novel. He wore a well-tailored grey suit with a double placket (a style that was a little fast, according to her mother). From the moment he entered Reception, it was clear that he was an important client. As soon as she rang through to announce his arrival, Hoskins came bustling out of his office to greet him. There was a pump-action handshake and a hefty slapping of shoulders before the office door shut behind them. Later, Hoskins escorted the client out and returned to his office, nodding and winking at Angela on his way past her desk. He told her that Nicholas Clarkson was *an important client.*

He certainly became important to me.

RACHEL 4

Waking each morning, Rachel still took a moment to make sense of the pattern of light on the bedroom walls. She was not in her Battersea flat, fourth floor of the mansion flat, ten minutes' walk from the park. She was in Priory Cottage, surrounded by fields in a wooded valley, two miles from the nearest village and half an hour from the town of Honiton, antique dealers' Mecca. Questions set in.

Had she really meant to move?

How was she to earn money?

Had she been over optimistic?

Would she make any friends?

Was her neighbour going to be a problem?

Would she ever get the cottage straight?

Would the second bedroom make a good enough studio?

What was Malcolm thinking, feeling? She very much hoped he was miserable without her.

Had she been out of her mind to change what had been a comfortable and secure life for a wild dash to Devon where her only friend was her brother? She'd turned her back on her publisher who was also her lover. Work and love! The two essentials in life. She'd left both. But whatever doubts she entertained, she knew she'd made the right decision. She had to to break free of her half-life with Malcolm. It had been a relationship that, in its very ease, stifled her. It led nowhere. Half-independence was worse than no independence at all. And as each year passed, her hope of having a family of her own receded. Nearing forty! She hardly dared count.

She'd made the move in time. Who knew what the future would hold for her? Listening to birdsong as she woke each morning, she told herself it would be good. The price, though, was high, both emotionally and financially. The last time she'd shopped – she hadn't bought anything particularly unusual or expensive – the bill had come to a sum that she didn't think was possible. She'd unpacked the bags on the kitchen table and carefully checked each item against the receipt. There'd been no mistake.

The onslaught of misgivings each morning lessened as the weeks past. Rachel worked hard at getting the cottage in a state that satisfied her. Walls became white. Floors were sanded, scrubbed; bleached. Curtains made. The kitchen dresser was a work in progress, banished to the lean-to outside the back door. She worked on the cottage, inside and out, in the mornings, hard labour interspersed with time at the computer. She systematically emailed artist's agents and every contact she could think of. She spent the afternoons exploring her surroundings. She bought an old bike with a wicker basket attached to the handlebars. She loved pedalling around the lanes, feeling the air sweep her hair from her forehead.

Betty Middleton picked her up on Saturday mornings to take her to the weekly market. Here she was getting to know a few of the regulars: Tessa with silverwork from India; Andy, home-made charcuterie; Phyllida, secondhand paperbacks; Linda, wickerwork, source of the basket on Rachel's bike. Each invited her to find them at home, and she circled the lanes, following signposts, crossing fords, taking No Through Roads. The countryside which had been a green desert of fields and woods became a place studded with the names of the people she'd met.

There came a time when Rachel felt steady enough in her new surroundings to invite her friend Sally to stay for a weekend. Sally was delighted and booked herself in for the very next weekend. Rachel would meet her at Exeter St David's on the Friday evening. "But isn't that miles away from you?" queried Sally.

"Yes. Everything is miles away from me. That's the blessing."

"I'd find it a curse."

Rachel hoped that the weekend would convince Sally that she'd made a good decision. They had been good friends so long that it was important to her that Sally approved, even if she did feel hurt and let down: Rachel had abandoned ship. So everything this weekend had to be perfect. She would show the countryside to the best advantage. Instead of taking the main road, she drove home from the station by the lanes; the picturesque route, she explained. But it was not a wise choice. It was growing late, and Sally was silent.

"There's a lovely view from here," Rachel announced as they reached the top of the hill out of the village. It was time to demonstrate that her present surroundings won, hands down, over Battersea Park.

She stopped the car at the field gate which gave onto the view. She often paused here on the bike, not just to get her breath back, but to wallow in the scene that Constable would have made famous had he lived here. From this point, the valley opened out below, a picture framed by hedgerow oaks. The jagged summit of the ivy-clad priory tower could be seen emerging from its thicket. The shining river, the cottage's thatched roof, Torridon's chimneys, and the Middletons' fields; all clustered in the centre of the valley, ringed by gently folding, wooded hills.

"I'm sure the view is lovely, if we could but see it," said Sally.

Fog was rising from the river. Very little could be made out in the gloaming. Rachel had to laugh. "You're right. But tomorrow! I'll show you everything, down to the very last blade of grass."

Next morning they appeared in the kitchen at much the same time, both groaning pitifully. They each blamed the other. Rachel accused Sally of bringing the sort of good quality wine that had to be tasted and tested at once. Sally replied that no force had been required to get Rachel to open three bottles.

"Three? Only two surely?"

Rachel wished to prove this was a gross exaggeration but saw, among the wreckage of dishes, left-overs, plates and glasses, there were two empty bottles on the table and a third opened. She turned away to look out of the window, beyond the sink where the washing-up bowl overflowed with food-encrusted saucepans and scummy water. What on earth had she cooked the day before? Anyone would think it was a banquet for 12, not a light supper for two. The garden presented a better view. The sun was picking out the copper coloured leaves of the bushes, still festooned with tangles of Old Man's beard, despite her and Oliver's efforts. She turned her attention back to Sally who looked like a graphic illustration of how she herself felt. "I'll make coffee. That's what I'll do. In just a moment."

Sally, using the table as support, sat down and carefully laid her head in her hands.

They had progressed no further than coffee when Betty Middleton appeared, knocking on the back door as she entered. "Oh! Your friend! I'd forgotten you were having a visitor." Her eyes roamed the kitchen, taking in the scene.

Rachel began to introduce Sally to Betty but found that the words she wanted weren't coming readily. In any case Betty was telling Sally all about the Saturday market - who was going to be there today – someone called Robert she was keen for Rachel to meet – and how well Rachel was settling in – and how nice it was for Betty and her husband Stan to have young company as their children were grown-up and busy with their own families now. And how happy she was to take them both to the Saturday market. There was plenty of room in her car, although today she only had her mini as Stan was taking the 4 by 4 to pick up a tumble dryer which she'd bought on Amazon Marketplace as theirs had gone bananas.

At this point there was a break long enough for Rachel to speak. "Thanks, Betty, but."

"But what? But nothing!" Betty was adamant that she drive Rachel and her friend to the village for the market. She took a lot of persuading that this was not going to happen. "Oh, alright then," she said in the end. "But bring Sally to the farm tomorrow, will you?"

"Obviously your new best friend," said Sally later. Betty had given up and gone, leaving Rachel to show Sally around the cottage. They were now climbing the narrow spiral staircase, on their way to the room which Rachel was turning into a studio.

"I know, but she's very kind and it's good to get on with your neighbours."

"And how's the one right next door? The one you thought you might have trouble with?"

"Actually, I hardly ever come across him. So it's fine." Rachel opened the door into her studio and regarded the room as though through Sally's eyes. She had her big table set up in front of the window, built under the eaves of the cottage roof. Bookshelves lined the wall to the right and on either side of the door. She'd unpacked most of her books. Her two large plan chests stood against the wall lined with pegboard. Her aim was to put up a display of her best illustrations on this wall, to show anyone who might commission her. She explained her plans to Sally who had moved to the table and was pushing folders aside. "Any possibilities yet?" asked Sally.

Rachel wasn't sure if she wanted Sally to see what she'd tucked beneath the pile.

"No, nothing from London which doesn't surprise me in the least. I'd drawn a blank before I left. The dearth helped me decide to make the break. I'm not like you, a dab hand with computer graphics. You still got masses of work?"

"Not exactly masses but enough. What's this, Ray?" Sally had plucked the sketch Rachel had hidden beneath the pile of folders.

"Oh, that's just an experiment at the moment."

"I can see something on its way. Pre-Raphaelite?"

"Not exactly." Rachel hesitated, as though at a traffic island in a busy road. If she couldn't confide in Sally, then in who else? All her ideas would stay in her own head and rot away. "It's very much the faintest of the slightest beginnings of an idea."

She moved to the window and looked down at the garden. From this window, she could see as far as the orchard which formed her boundary to the field beyond. To the right, over the chaos of overgrowth which hid all but a small section of broken fence, she could see the untamed wilderness of Clarkson's garden, through which she sometimes caught a glimpse of him coming from or going to his workshop, an ugly, prefabricated concrete block just visible in a thick copse of willow and hazel. The workshop was backed by a band of conifers that hid the priory ruins and the source of her inspiration.

She took the piece of sketching paper from Sally and regarded what she had drawn objectively. The languid young women she'd roughed out, their profiles appearing through haloes of ringlets, were on the right lines, she thought. The style of their garments, roughly filled in with a wash of watercolour, pointed in the right direction. She felt she could bring Elfrida to life on the page, but she needed to hear Sally's encouragement. It could turn out a total waste of time. "What do you think?"

"Well, I can't really tell yet. What have you in mind?"

"*Elfrida was a maid so pure,*" quoted Rachel, still unsure how much to explain to Sally.

"And what on earth is that supposed to mean?"

"It's a ballad. A ballad that was among the cottage's papers. It's about a young girl called Elfrida. She's rather got under my skin. She lived in the 13th century. Spent her life here - well, not in this cottage – but in the priory. I'm thinking of illustrating the ballad in an illuminated manuscript kind of way."

Sally looked doubtful. "Well, I think you could do anything you wanted. Has the wicked warthog really come to end? Surely you could continue from down here?"

Rachel was hurt and surprised that Sally hadn't understood how totally she'd left London. "I'm not here on an extended holiday, whatever you may think. I cut off absolutely all contact with Malcolm and the firm when I left London. I was sick of Walter Warthog in any case."

"And sick of the fees?"

"I still get royalties. And I'm simply doing what you've been telling me to do for years. Prune my life, to let the light in."

"I've never used such a horticultural expression."

"No, that's me in my new life. *Cypress leylandii.* You see? That's the name of the hedge around the parking space."

"Deeply impressed," said Sally.

"I'll let you read the poem later. The thing that excites me is that it's not fantasy stuff for children. Elfrida is real. I mean, was. Was real. She lived the life of a hermit, sealed up a cell in the priory. Down there!" She pointed out of the window.

Sally joined her at the window. She gave an exaggerated shudder. "How grim! Can you get into the cell? Does it still exist?"

"I'm not sure."

"Haven't you looked?"

Rachel hesitated. How could she tell Sally that she didn't like to ask her neighbour for anything. To request an invitation into his garden to see the ruins was beyond contemplation. "It's a little tricky," she said at last. She wished she could put into words her reaction to Clarkson but she barely understood it herself. Was it she or he who was avoiding contact? Considering the parking space between the houses was mutual territory, it was extraordinary that they coincided there so seldom. When they did happen to meet, their exchanges were pleasant but truncated to a word or two about the weather. Clarkson seemed as keen as she was to get away.

"He's not an easy character." She began to elaborate but Sally's eyes were gleaming at her.

"He's fallen for you!"

"No! Not a bit of it. You're way off course!"

"Why should he be an exception? People are always falling for you. You told me he's single."

"Yes, but you've got it all wrong. He doesn't want to have anything to do with me. A normal neighbour would have invited a newcomer in. I haven't set foot into Torridon."

"He's obviously shy. After all, you can be intimidating. I expect you stand out a bit round here. You're still a Londoner."

Rachel thought this was grossly unfair. She thought she blended into the countryside as though born and bred here. Before she could object, Sally continued. "And I bet you're taller than he is, which is never a good start for a romantic relationship."

"I may be taller – I have no idea, actually, we haven't stood long enough in the same spot! Anyrate, he's *not* after me. He's just – absorbed in his own things." That explained him well enough for the moment. But Sally wasn't satisfied.

"What are his own things?"

"Actually, I know very little about him."

"What? No curiosity? That's unlike you."

Rachel frowned, trying to recall any snippets of information she'd been given. The truth was that she was not interested in Clarkson. He was not the sort of man she'd moved out of London to meet. All she could tell Sally was the fact that his wife had left him – or had she died? He was a business man who'd retired early and he dealt in antiques – and he did carpentry - or was it metalwork? - in the shed at the bottom of his garden. "

"But you are interested in the hermit's cell, aren't you," said Sally. "I'd like to see it, too. Let's go and knock on his door and ask to see the ruins. Is there anything wrong with that?"

Rachel found it impossible to muster any persuasive arguments against this plan. Her antipathy to Clarkson rested on nothing more solid than a vague feeling of unease. Sally's wishes prevailed; so, later in the morning, she found herself leading her across the parking space, through the conifer archway to Torridon's front door. There was no knocker and no bell visible. She raised her hand to knock.

"Why are you so nervous?" Sally spoke in an undertone.

"I'm not!" mouthed Rachel. Sally's eyes were gleaming with the wrong assumptions. "I have no interest in him whatsoever." She knocked on the door firmly.

They waited.

"Is he out, do you think?" asked Sally.

"We could check the barn where he keeps his car." She spoke in a whisper. She imagined Nicolas hovering just the other side of his front door.

After a moment, Sally stood back and made as though to go around to the back of the house.

"Stop!" hissed Rachel. "Don't!" She grabbed Sally's arm before she'd gone more than a few yards. "We can't!"

The front door opened at this moment. Clarkson stood in the doorway, his eyes on the two women as they stopped and turned. "Can I help you?" he asked, with no glimmer of recognition.

Rachel felt as though she'd been caught trespassing. Holding Sally by the arm, she pulled her back to the front door, hearing herself utter a stupid jumble of explanations. "Just wondering ...in or out ...Sally ... this is ....friend staying.... Priory ... wants to see ...could we?"

"Ah," said Clarkson, moving onto the front step and closing the door behind him. "It's Rachel. Good morning." His politely spoken greeting sounded like a rebuke.

"So! Sorry! Yes," She gathered herself together. "Good morning. May I introduce - "

"Sally," interrupted Clarkson. "I heard the first time." He

held out his hand.

Sally gave him her wide-mouthed, cheerful smile as they shook hands.

Don't smile at him! thought Rachel.

"You want to see the ruins?"

"Yes, please. Can we? I understand they are at the bottom of your garden."

The thing about Sally, thought Rachel, was that she always assumed people would give her what she wanted, with the result that people did give her what she wanted.

"They are."

"I'm so interested in the priory's history."

"Are you?"

"Yes. And Rachel is, too."

"Many people are, of course," said Nicolas coldly.

"So you get many visitors?"

"No. None."

"Why is that?" Sally could get at the truth of things.

Rachel struggled to think of a way they could retreat before the situation grew worse; worse in a way she could not imagine.

"We don't want to bother you," she put in hastily.

Clarkson turned to her. He seemed to be re-evaluating her. What was he thinking? It was impossible to guess.

"No bother," he said. "No, not at all." He smiled. It was more a demonstration that he had a set of evenly-spaced, white teeth. His eyes glittered beneath a brow which bore a frown that looked as though it was carved in marble. He unnerved Rachel in a way she could not understand.

There was a second or two of silence. Then Rachel and Sally spoke at once.

Rachel said they were on their way to the Middletons, while Sally said that they didn't need him to show them round, they'd just have a little wander by themselves.

"It's too dangerous," said Nicholas.

Dangerous? Rachel shrank into herself. How could he know that she was thinking the word applied to him?

"In what way exactly?" asked Sally.

"Ruins are dangerous. Unstable ground. Piles of stones. You could fall down a hole."

"Oh, we'd be very careful," said Sally.

"You might be careful but the fact of the matter is I don't allow visitors."

"Oh, what a shame," said Sally but she didn't sound as though she'd give up.

Rachel slipped her hand under Sally's elbow. "Off we go then. We've lots of people to see."

Sally spoke at the same time. "A glance, then? It must be just beyond your workshop? Is there a viewpoint?

"No, there isn't. And if you don't mind, I am very busy this morning. So I'll wish you good-day." He opened his front door just wide enough to slip back inside.

"You're right. An odd man," said Sally on their way to Rachel's car.

Rachel was relieved. They were now free to visit some of the nice, normal people she'd met in the neighbourhood. And they could have a pub lunch in the village first.

ANGELA 5

Sometimes, on a good day – and there are good days every now and again – I can close my eyes and re-create a scene from the past. Today I find I am back in London, in my first and only job.

I'm 20 years old and the new client comes in, with a little rush of fresh air. He leans on my desk. I notice the small hairs that spring up on the backs of his hands. Even the short sections between the joints of his fingers bear a sprinkling of bristling, brown hair. This fascinates me. I listen to his voice and imagine him singing hymns in church, or delivering a sermon. He has authority.

At the time, I'm going out with Nigel from home. My parents called him "poor Nigel" because he was always hanging around the rectory, hoping I was free to go for a walk. I didn't want to go for a walk with Nigel. At the same time, I didn't want to be horrid to him. It took all my ingenuity to avoid having to say an outright no. That would be lovely, I'd say; but I have loads of homework today. The next time I'd come up with another excuse about essays, or maths tests. He'd left school the year before, so this was a safe thing to plead. I think in the year Nigel hung around I only went for a walk with him once. Along the river. It was completely boring.

The first time I went out with Nicolas it was not in the least boring. It was thrilling. He took me to a restaurant in Soho which had linen tablecloths and napkins. The waiter lit the candle on the table. Nicolas studied the wine list, keeping up a commentary about French vineyards. Fortunately, he didn't seem to expect any response from me. I was way out of my depth. This was light years away from the Chinese my parents took me to on my birthdays. Of course I was thrilled.

I used to wonder what Nicolas saw in me. It's only lately that I've seen the situation more objectively. I was malleable. An ideal sop for his ego. I know I wasn't unattractive. I had a good figure and beautiful eyes, or so people told me. My hair had come right, thanks to a clever cut that made it somehow curve around my face and tilt for-

ward at jawline. (If I could see it now --- rats' tails, it feels like). That first time out, Nicolas leant across the table and said something about losing himself in twin pools of blue water. I ask you! I lapped it up.

Not long after this, I introduced him to my parents. He was nearly 40 and seemed elderly; in fact, closer in age to them than to me. He's always been good with people who have something he wants. Engagement and marriage – it all happened fast. Nicolas hurries on to the next thing. Perhaps he didn't want to give me time to think too hard about the difference in our ages. And I didn't want to think about anything negative. I, too, wanted to hurry on. The picture of being a married woman without any worries about making a living was alluring. No more taking dictation from Hoskins. Bliss!

When did I start to have misgivings? Hard to tell from this standpoint. I like to think I wised up soon, but no, I know I didn't. Not at all. When I consulted a counsellor after our silver wedding anniversary, it was like having cotton wool removed from my eyes. I can't remember exactly what she said, but it was about jigsaw pieces and it made absolute sense. Generally speaking, we fit each other's characters neatly, in all our shapes and sizes. If one piece is overpowering, the other is underpowering. If one piece changes, then what happens? You no longer fit. Something has to give or you split apart. Sitting in the therapist's room, the realisation came to me. I'd let Nicolas bully me from the very start.

That was shortly before I ordered from John Lewis the wooden block holding a set of kitchen knives. Even now, at this distance, I feel the rush of terror at the sight of them, unpacked on the kitchen table. A sudden removal of stability A trap door opens under your feet. The lift goes down. The onset of vertigo. All the same, I did not imagine ever being driven to the point of using a knife as a weapon.

RACHEL 5

The pottery studio was full of noise and people. Tina was holding an autumn sale over the weekend and this presented Rachel with an opportunity for showing Sally that not everyone in the neighbourhood was as weird as Clarkson.

They moved around the studio together but soon parted company, gravitating to different displays of pottery. Sally wanted to look at, and possibly buy, mugs. Rachel wanted something to put flowers in. After a while Rachel looked around for Sally and saw her sitting on a low-slung sofa in animated conversation with the sofa's other occupants – a man and a woman who Rachel hadn't yet come across and who looked interesting. Sally was talking animatedly, fluttering her hands. Her feet rested on Tina's springer spaniel. Rachel couldn't hear what she was saying, but it clearly entertained the two sitting on either side of her. She went over to join them.

Sally glanced up with a smile and the conversation continued. Rachel perched on the arm of the sofa and tuned in. They were talking about the priory ruins; she could only pick up a word or two amidst the general hubbub in the room. Then she realised that Sally was telling the couple about her ideas for the Elfrida story. She quickly intervened. "No, no, there's nothing as definite as that yet! It's just a vague idea at the moment."

"It sounds really intriguing." The woman at the far end of the sofa leant forward to look at Rachel. "Our children love Walter! This will be brilliant."

"No!" Rachel was quick to put this impression right. "It won't be anything like Walter. More like an illuminated manuscript as imitated by a pre-Raphaelite. If you see what I mean. But I don't know if I can. Early days yet."

The man sitting in the middle depths of the sofa struggled to his feet. "Take my seat. I should have a look round." He stood in front of her, his hands on the small of his back.

"This is Rob," said Sally. She glanced up at him. "Or do you prefer Robert?"

"Either is fine. I don't really notice what I'm called."

"And this is." But she hadn't yet learnt the name.

"Lucy," supplied Rob.

The woman in the far corner of the sofa tucked in her chin and looked at Rachel with a small, sidelong smile. Big blue eyes. Long, crinkly fair hair, even features, demure – in fact, thought Rachel with a thrill, she looked almost exactly like her idea of Elfrida. She'd get in touch with Lucy another day and see if she couldn't do some sketches of her.

"Rob does wrought iron. He makes things like weathervanes. And Lucy works at home – twins and a baby, all under five. Imagine! You'd like a weathervane, wouldn't you, Rachel? I'll give you one for Christmas. How about that? Something to do with the priory perhaps? What could it be? Robert, any ideas?"

Robert straightened. It clearly hurt him. "Christ," he said, "Tina's sofa. It's a danger to mankind." His eyes engaged directly with hers. "You may not want to take my place."

Rachel was the first to look away. Something was stirring within her. She got to her feet unsteadily. She hadn't experienced the sensation of inner upheaval for a long time, but she recognised it at once. She likened it to shifting sands. At first glance, for goodness's sake! And another attached man! Absolutely not.

"Or do you?" questioned Robert.

"Do I what?"

He gestured towards the sofa's vacant place.

"No." she said, too abruptly. "No, thanks. I shall have a look around, too."

She shouldn't have said "too". She set off quickly to make it clear that she wasn't inviting him on a joint tour of the pottery. When she saw him leave the studio after a few minutes, she returned to the sofa to talk to the Elfrida look-alike.

"Weren't they nice," said Sally later over lunch in the pub. "I was serious about the weathervane idea. I'd like to have a little more to do with that hunk of a blacksmith. Wouldn't you?"

"No I wouldn't. Give me a break. No more involvements for years and years, thank you."

"Okay, then. Leave him for me!"

"Certainly!"

But she had to admit to Sally that she'd be seeing more of Lucy. "I've asked her if I could sketch her sometime. For Elfrida." She'd been enthusiastic about Rachel's ideas. She'd also given her Robert's business card on which she scribbled their home phone number.

"Oh, you're right. She *is* Elfrida! You must do that. And I would really like to commission Robert to make you a weathervane. Next time I'm down, let's visit his forge and talk it over."

"I don't think that's a good idea."

Sally regarded her with an exaggeratedly questioning expression, pulling down her mouth at the corners and twitching her eyebrows.

She thought of a reason. "Thatched roofs don't have weathervanes."

"Why on earth not?"

But she couldn't think why not. Besides, the idea of visiting Robert in his workshop and having him make something for her was beginning to override her caution. Now she'd recognised the effect he had on her, she could stay immune. It was simply a matter of controlling her responses. As soon as she felt a quiver, she would say to herself *London*! That would be shorthand for all the mistakes she'd made in the past and prevent her repeating them in the future.

If she was to sketch Lucy, then she'd be visiting their home, which she understood was next door to the forge. She'd probably be saying *London* a lot.

At the station, they got out their diaries to agree the date of Sally's next visit when they would visit the forge and discuss a design.

"You contact Rob," said Rachel. "You fix the time with him."

"I need his email, then, and phone number."

Rachel gave her Robert's card. It showed a weathervane decorated with the model of a fox. "What about a greyhound?" Sally suggested as she got on the train.

Rachel had drawn Elfrida with a hand laid on the head of a greyhound on the pad she'd brought to the pub. Long, narrow, tall, thin; elongated, sinuous; glowing, gold leaf, emerald green, ultramarine, scarlet - those were among the words she used to describe her visions of the illustrated poem.

"Greyhound! Good!" called Rachel, as the train began to move. She could see a greyhound-shaped weathervane on the peak of the thatched roof above her studio, a black metal shape against the sky, turned towards the priory at the bottom of Clarkson's garden. But only, of course, when the wind was coming from that direction.

ANGELA 6

Nicolas didn't so much propose marriage as assume it. And that was on the basis of one kiss after our third meal out together. As Marilou, my counsellor - she came from Iowa – helped me see, I was as much in a hurry to become a married woman as Nicolas was to make me his wife. My parents, too, were eager to see their only daughter in a stable financial situation. I suggested to Marilou that they could take some of the blame for what I suffered as his wife. But she wasn't having that. She may not have put it in as many words but in her quiet, mostly silent way, she made me realise that we are each responsible for our own actions and must live with the consequences.

So I take responsibility for everything that has happened since that first kiss. It came out of the blue and it was nothing like Nigel's hopeful but useless fumblings. Nicolas was firm and straightforward. I was in the passenger seat of his car and we were driving back into London after a meal in a pub in Kent. At traffic lights, he put an arm around me and pulled me towards his chest. I remember what he said as his face came closer. "I have to kiss you." Have to! The inevitability was bewitching. I'd been enthralled before that, though. From the moment he'd placed his two hands on my desk and looked at me with an intensity I'd never before come across, I was his to do what he liked with.

The lights changed. Nicolas drove on. The next time he took me out for a meal, he was talking of a future in which "we" took centre stage. Looking back it seems like a conjuring trick. I cannot for the life of me remember a time when his plans didn't include me. And how happily I went along with it!

What I want to do now is track the time I began to resent the control – or at least to realise what was making me depressed. That is, over and above my two miscarriages which happened during our first five years of marriage.

I find it hard to concentrate. The drip has started again. The green stain is spreading around it. The mark I make at its edge is the fourth. I have a sharp stone to score the walls. Without any verification outside my own mind, marks show me the passage of time. I should have started at the beginning, but I didn't think I would be here any time at all.

Depression. Loss of autonomy. When did I realise how Nicolas exercised control over me?

I think it was after we'd moved to Torridon.

He looked on the Victorian house as a transplanted laird's domain, befitting a man descended on his mother's side from a chieftain of the MacDonald clan. Torridon is a place in Scotland, apparently. He made the best of being called Clarkson, a thoroughly English name, although every so often he looked into the business of changing it to MacDonald. I know that because I learnt how to track his search history on his computer, having discovered his password: I only took advantage of this a couple of times, because usually I was terrified he'd come back to check on me before he'd barely left. He often did this, driving out to the lane, turning around and returning, carefully opening and shutting the gates out and in and out again. What determination! What neurosis! And what a bother! I'd watch him from the landing window, through the horrible net curtain he insisted must hang in that big window. He thought the Johnsons next door spent their hours glued to the only window in the cottage which faced in our direction, looking out for movements in Torridon. I ask you. Every time he went out, I always gave myself time to watch from the landing window. If I saw him coming back down the track, I'd make sure I was peeling a potato or coring an apple or doing something in the kitchen when he looked in at the front door.

"Back so soon?" I'd call out, in all innocence.

"Forgot my ...-" and he'd fill in whatever he thought of at the time. Keys. Briefcase. Umbrella. Sunglasses. Diary. Poor man. He was permanently unhappy. Do I still feel sorry for him? The guard is as much of a prisoner as a prisoner is, when you come to think of it. If only he'd gone to Marilou when I suggested it. But he'd never do *that, because there was nothing the matter with him. The fault lay in other people. In the whole world.*

Not a happy life for either of us. I should have left him years ago. Easier said than done. If I had my life again, I would be stronger, more determined.

The trouble is: I was always afraid of hurting his feelings. Isn't that absurd. Better to be hurt, than to hurt another. Rectory-speak. Yet there was surely another way, if I could have found it.

RACHEL 6

For several nights after the weekend when Sally had stayed, Rachel didn't sleep well. Thoughts flickered in and out of her head behind her determinedly closed eyelids. Her eyes felt as though they'd been coated in sandpaper and tightly locked into their sockets. She fought for sleep to take over, and then fought the fight itself, clenching and unclenching her muscles as people recommended. She wiggled her ankles, made cups of tea and raided the biscuit tin. She kept a notebook by her bed to capture anything useful but nothing came to mind which could be expressed in a note. She saw oddments of written words and images. Silly scraps. The sagging sofa in Tina's pottery studio. The chap who'd got to his feet and looked down on her with smiling eyes. She tried to hear his voice. It was the kind of voice she liked. I don't notice what I'm called, he'd said. An interesting thought. Did she herself notice what she was called? Sally sometimes called her Ray, and she liked that. The dog by the studio sofa had a name, but what was it? Sally wanted to commission a greyhound weathervane from the tall man. His name came to her. Bob. Or was it Rob? Robert. Taffy was the woolly-coated mongrel she'd rested her feet on. Taffy was a Welshman, Taffy was a thief. The Queen liked Welsh corgis. The fact had appeared in a crossword clue. An anagram. The mongrel was far too long-legged to have any corgi in him. Who did he belong to? Tina the potter, or the couple on the sofa? Rob and someone who looked like the Elfrida of her imagination. She was called Lucy. Lucy's face appeared; the face she wanted to draw. Millais's Ophelia. The story she'd write in chunky black calligraphy to be set around the illustrations. She'd make the paintings look like an illuminated manuscript. Or like icons painted on rough wooden blocks. Would it be best to glue on sheets of gold leaf, use gesso, or dip a brush in a bottle of gold leaf paint, the hairs of her brush sticky with it?

Elfrida had been raped.

Possibly she'd just been asleep but now she was fully awake again. Elfrida's story was NOT suitable material for a children's book. Why hadn't that occurred to her before? Elfrida was haunting her. She could see a willowy damsel with flowing hair held back with a ribbon, shown sideview with black inked Latin words fitted above and to the side of the image; hunc hic est; Latin words interspersed with English words telling her story. She'd have to do a lot of research. She saw herself having lunch with Oliver in Exeter; she'd visit the Cathedral library; surely there'd be something there. Oliver had told her the library held the original text of the south western contributions to the Domesday Book. That was produced in the 11th century, well before Elfrida's day. '1066 and all that' was the title of a jokey, mock-historical book. She'd have to be careful to find the right tone and atmosphere for hers. Not a children's book; of course not. But what sort of book? She saw a small pile near a bookshop's till. A Christmas present. Beautifully drawn, beautifully produced. Who would publish it?

Her mind turned to London and she felt a swift wave of sick regret, quickly banished. She was not going to hark back to her break with Malcolm. Better to have no future as a book illustrator than to be stuck in a relationship with no future. She'd start work on Elfrida's book and leave any thoughts of outcome until it was finished. If money got tight, she'd take up the job she'd been offered by Tony, the pub's landlord.

She felt herself drifting. She was drawing a picture of a knight in armour sitting on a horse while she wiped ring marks from the top of a table in the pub. She woke and knew she'd slept. Coffee and a plan for the day. All was well.

Lucy was surprised and flattered when Rachel asked if she could call in with her sketch pad sometime soon. "No-one has ever wanted to draw me before!" she said. "But to be honest, I wouldn't be a good model. I have great bags under my eyes and

I'll never be able to sit still long enough. You know there are three children under five in this household? When the oldest is at school and the middle one at nursery I'm catching up at home with the baby and housework and shopping and washing and god knows what."

Rachel, listening to this, was relieved yet again that she'd never had children, even while feeling a familiar twinge of jealousy.

"I could come over when they're in bed," she suggested, "or at a weekend?" She realised, as she spoke, that she was being prompted by the little demon of interest in Robert, a demon that must be squashed.

"I don't think that would work."

Why not, Rachel wondered. Was Lucy too accustomed to female visitors being interested in her husband? She could imagine this might be the case and gave up the idea of Lucy as an Elfrida model. Maybe this was for the best. It was like locking the last packet of cigarettes in a drawer so as not to break her vow to stop smoking. She would not think about Robert. Instead she turned her attention to finding another model. She sat in a corner of the pub, reading a newspaper while keeping a sharp eye out for the right profile. No-one suitable materialised.

A couple of weeks later she received a phone call. A male voice she didn't recognize said that he'd heard she was after a model for some illustrations she was doing.

Her spirits rose. A London agent perhaps? "Sorry, I didn't catch your name."

"Rob. We met at Tina's pottery."

She felt as though she'd taken a blow in her midriff. His voice went on but she couldn't make sense of what he was saying.

"Sorry. Could you say that again?"

He repeated that he'd heard she wanted Lucy to model. "You mustn't take her no for an answer. It's her natural response to any question. A safety mechanism to give her time to consider. She'd actually love it if she modelled for Walter the Warthog's creator."

"Oh but it won't be like that. Not a children's book at all. More like the sort of book you give a friend for a special birthday."

"Ah. Am I right in thinking it has something to do with the priory legend?"

"Yes. Do you know the Elfrida story? The ballad?"

He did. He explained that Ruth Johnson was a cousin of his mother's and she'd often talked of the priory and the 13th-century nun.

This silenced Rachel. It was almost as if Rob had moved into Priory Cottage. She was glad when he was ready to ring off with a promise that he would get Lucy to fix a time for Rachel to call in with her sketch pad.

She put the phone back on her desk and gazed out of the window unseeingly. Elfrida, in the shape of Lucy, was drawing closer. So, dangerously so, was Rob. He'd sounded warm and friendly. Overwarm, overfriendly? He'd even said something about calling in on her one day, to tell her more about Priory Cottage. How had she answered that? She felt she'd hardly said a word throughout the whole conversation. He must think her a dumb fool. But she guessed from his tone of voice that this was not the case.

Perhaps, if he did call in one day, there'd be no harm in that. She had lots of friends who were male without there being the remotest thought of anything further. Rob would make a good friend, she was certain of that. She let this encouraging view stay with her for a moment or two.

But maybe it was different in the countryside? What would people think if Rob became a good friend? She was single. He had Lucy and three children! She imagined the kind of disapproval that would emanate from, say, the Middletons' kitchen.

She mustn't encourage any "callings in". Besides, he was surely too busy. His family life and the forge must fill his days. She persuaded herself that he wouldn't.

The next day, though, she heard a knock on the front door. She went quickly from her upstairs studio to look out of the landing window. It was not Clarkson, her first thought. It was Rob. He'd stepped back from the porch and was looking up at the cottage, as though searching for signs of life. She became a useless teenager, spinning around the landing, trying to decide what to do. Check her face in the mirror? Change her clothes? Not answer? Hide? She heard him call out, tentatively. "Anyone at home?"

She went downstairs, all her misgivings crowding in on her. Rob was hesitating at the half-open door.

"A bad time?"

"No, fine."

"Working away?"

She heard herself making no sense as she led him into the kitchen. No, she wasn't working; yes, she was, but it didn't matter; she liked to be disturbed; no, he wasn't disturbing her; she was about to make coffee; no, she wasn't; she was working, he could come in just for a moment; no, she didn't mean that; he could stay as long as he liked; she wasn't working on anything important.

"But you must have worked for hours on this," he said, his hand on the kitchen dresser. "You've got rid of all Ruth Johnson's black varnish."

"It did take a while."

"Worth it. You've done a marvellous job."

She didn't want to be praised for working for hours on a piece of furniture. She wanted to tell him all about her Elfrida ideas. At the same time, she knew she must damp down on her tendency to entertain, amuse, enthuse. She felt as though she was losing her footing on a steep slope. *Be cool, aloof*. That was what she had to be.

He'd brought a folder which he now opened and withdrew a red exercise book. "Some notes Ruth Johnson wrote about the history of the priory."

"Oh! How marvellous! Really? Can I read this?"

"That's why I brought it."

"How brilliant! Thank you!" Her hands were already flipping through the pages The lines were filled with blue ink handwriting which slanted forwards, trailing generous loops and twirls. There were also a number of small drawings of Gothic arches and ground plans. "Oo, what a feast!"

She didn't realise, until Rob left an hour later, how quickly and easily her resolution to be cool and distant had come undone.

ANGELA 7

    I like to recall the food I used to cook. Nicolas's mother Amy – Amy! Love! What a misnomer - gave me a recipe book which I liked, although I didn't like his mother. She wanted me to make the fruit cake she'd always made Nicolas for his birthday. "<u>And</u> iced it," she unfailingly added, underlining my inability to make icing of the right consistency. Royal or fondant, it made no difference which sort of icing I intended to make: it was either too brittle, a hazard to our teeth, or so soft that it pooled on the plate, running off the cake like a river over a rock. I can hear Nicolas asking for a teaspoon. I think he meant us to laugh.

    Nicolas's birthday cake was imaginatively called The Best Fruit Cake Ever and the recipe was on page 67. I often felt like ripping the page out of the book because it cast a long shadow over the other pages. But I wanted to keep the book intact, despite my dislike of the book's giver. Some recipes I followed faithfully. Others I simply read. There was one I often read and never followed. It involved three different kinds of meat. Cubes of pork, steak and lamb layered with onion and stewed slowly in stock for five hours. A Finnish dish. It made me think of snow and ice and hunkering down in an igloo while the casserole hung over a central fire. You'd be glad the casserole took five hours to cook.

    Serves 8, so it said. But we never had eight people to feed. The most we ran to was six: Nicolas's parents, his sister and her husband, and ourselves. That came to end early on in our marriage. His parents died one after the other, and his sister and husband moved to Canada. I had imagined we would then see more of our friends and entertain them to meals. But no, Nicolas said we had no need to feed anyone else. They could come in for drinks at six o'clock and then go home to their own suppers. Well, that saved me some anxiety over the question who to invite and what to cook. After a few years, even the numbers at our infrequent drinks parties dwindled. When we moved to Torridon, the Johnsons would come in from next door - thank heaven, such a lovely couple even if immensely old. They'd leaven the company of the other three: Megan who groomed dogs, Avril the disgruntled white Rhodesian (she wouldn't refer to Zimbabwe) and Charlie, a software developer with an uncontrollable stammer. Yes, you can imagine. Difficult. Eventually I realised – how thick I was! It took me years! – that it wasn't my fault we had so few friends.

I've been going over and over this. At what point did I realise that it was **Nicolas** that people found difficult? What brought it home to me?

I suppose I actually hero-worshipped him at the beginning. He was much older, and far more important. I was nothing. Yet he paid me attention, took me out to dinner in a posh restaurant and proposed to me! Of course I'd do anything for him. He knew about tipping the waiter, which wine to order, what to think of the government, what I should wear, what we should eat, where we should go on holiday, if we should have a holiday at all, what I should do while he played golf on Saturdays. Now it comes back to me --- he even told me how to answer the phone! Don't say Hello. Say your name first and then how can I help you? If – as it always was – someone who wanted to speak to Nicolas, I was expected to write down their name and number and say that he would call them back. The need to be seen as important and busy overrode the addition to the phone bill, even when Nicolas was within yards of the phone. I wasn't to ask why they wanted to speak to him; heavens no. Even if the subject had some bearing on me and my time; for instance, the plumber calling about the boiler check. I would know Dave wanted to arrange a time and day, yet I had to follow the etiquette. That was Nicolas's word for the rigmarole. He with his background (father a solicitor) knew about etiquette which I with mine (impoverished vicar of a small parish) didn't. At some level I knew this was a false summary of our relative backgrounds. His mother talked of settees rather than sofas – just imagine the niceties of our English social levels! Do the Germans or the French have such subtle gradations? I don't think to quite the same extreme, but that's another subject to think about another time. I can hear the distant door grind open. Now will follow the *series of noises that serve me as geography. Metallic clanging, thuds, squeaks – from what I imagine is an intervening hallway between outside and me, though I could be wrong. The noises come closer until finally my door opens and Nicolas appears for the routine exchange of full and empty containers. I can voice requests which may or may not be met. I only bother to do this when I feel the need to hear my own voice, exercise my vocal chords. Sometimes Nicolas actually comes in "for a chat". Most times he stays outside.*

Today, bless me, he comes in.

RACHEL 7

"Could you perhaps lay your hand flat on the table as though you're resting it on the head of a dog?"

"Do you want a dog? We can manage that."

"No, I don't think that will help at this stage. Another time maybe." Did they have a dog as well as three children? Rachel didn't like the thought of having an animal to contend with as well as everything else. Since her arrival at the carefully negotiated time of 10.30 for an hour's session, she'd spent almost twenty minutes waiting for Lucy to settle the baby, throw breakfast things into the sink, and clear a space at the kitchen table for the two of them to sit. Fortunately, there was no dog in evidence. On the other hand ...

"What sort of dog do you have? I have a whippet or a greyhound in mind for Elfrida."

Lucy laughed delightedly. "An Irish wolfhound!"

"Oh heavens. Aren't they as tall as a man when they stand on their hind feet?"

"Yes. Don't worry, I was only teasing. Bob takes neighbourhood dogs for walks, and he does have an Irish wolfhound in his care. But we have a springer spaniel. Bob's got him this morning. He's such a handful."

Silence resumed. As directed, Lucy gazed down demurely at her hand lying on the table. Rachel's pencil flew over the page in her largest sketch book. Her aim was to catch the important lines in Lucy's profile: her nose which was not exactly a beak but getting on that way; a Roman nose, it could be called; full lips, long eyelashes, high cheek bones, smooth brow. A long lock of wavy blonde hair drew a half-moon around her face, before falling on her shoulders. In the quick lines she'd drawn so far, Rachel could see the Elfrida she wanted to create. She held her pencil loosely. It was a matter of maintaining intense concentration alongside a willingness to let her pencil find its own way.

If she could pull it off, the result would be a portrait of a hybrid between Lucy and her imagined Elfrida. Perhaps three sessions would be enough. As she progressed, she'd build up glimpses of the head, hair, shoulders, dress and eventually she'd have a full-length drawing to finish up in the studio.

Lucy was murmuring a question.

Rachel looked at her and saw Lucy rather than Elfrida. "Sorry. Did you say something?"

"Only just that I was wondering how it's coming along? I can hear Mattie."

"Mattie?"

"The baby."

"Oh bother!" Had the hour gone already?

"It's after eleven. I'm afraid we started late. I have such a tight schedule."

"Oh of course. I know. It's awfully good of you to spare the time."

"Can I see?"

"Oh no, not yet. There's nothing to see." She'd need twice as long to get anywhere with this.

"But you have done something? It's been useful?"

"Absolutely brilliant, thank you so, *so* much."

"No need to thank me. Enforced inactivity is exactly what I need." She jumped up from the table. As she left the kitchen, Rachel became aware of the sound of desperate, infant need. She realised the wailing had been growing in intensity, voicing demands which nature intended to be answered at once. Even she, who'd never been a mother, wanted to give the baby what it wanted, immediately.

Back home, she poured herself a glass of wine which she took upstairs to her studio, thanking her lucky stars she had no babies. But no lucky stars had been involved at all; simply her own wise, and almost unconsciously made, decision. It came to her - and not for the first time - that perhaps she'd remained an adjunct to Malcolm's life, as a safety net against autonomy. If she'd been on her own, making up her own independent life, she could well have fallen for a man who wanted a family with her. There had been one or two such men in the offing, but she'd always made clear the permanence of her relationship with Malcolm. Yet now she'd left him. Too late for babies. Too late for another love?

But there was time for Elfrida. Her own kind of book. She'd use acrylic paint on heavyweight paper. She looked at the rough drawings in her sketch book. She felt excited. She'd made a start! Now it was time to plan ahead. A list was needed. She pulled a brand new spiral bound notebook towards her, and picked up the pen with which she'd been experimenting with italic writing. She dipped it in the brand-new pot of black Indian ink.

Research, she wrote.

Practise italic writing.

Exeter library. Lunch with Oliver.

Look at Ruth Johnson's notebook.

Ask Lucy if she has an Elfrida-sort of dress to wear next session.

Talk more with Bob.

She scratched out the last item with such vigour that the nib of her italic pen pierced the paper and ink spattered onto her open sketch book, forming blobs on Lucy's nose and lips. She tried not to think this was a bad omen.

ANGELA 8

When I say "little chat" I don't mean a little chat. It's what Nicolas calls his long monologues. Every so often he needs to unwind the things that have lain tangled in his head for too long. Not that he himself admits the tangle; it's how I hear it. The same grudges appear, one mixed up with another. It can be hard to distinguish who said or did what to thwart him at different times. Often it's still me – even in this cell! - who's been the stupid one, who's stopped him in his tracks, argued, gone on too long, not listened to him, flown off the handle. While he – according to him – is always the very soul of reason. He considers himself to be a calm and logical person. Nobody else is as calm and logical as he is. I ask you!

Breathe, says Marilou. Yes, a deep breath. I mustn't work myself up into a useless rage. Still, just for a moment, back to the recent little chat…

The subjects that have lain waiting to be untangled lie not just in the recent past, but go back years. I long ago became adept at letting it all slide over me. In the beginning, I was keen to respond, either with a helpful comment about a work issue or to defend myself. But I soon learnt two things. First: I had only to open my mouth at the slightest pause and he'd plough on, talking over me. I put this down as my fault. My voice was too quiet. Second: if I tried to defend my behaviour, whatever I was accused of, he'd go wild. Result: I remained silent. Even silence was wrong, though. "For god's sake, don't just sit there like a pudding! Say something!" Sometimes he'd seize my shoulders and shake me in a way that frightened me. I perfected a variety of murmurs in tones rising and falling, shorter and longer, louder and softer, implying sympathy, sorrow, apology, agreement, shock. Whatever's appropriate. And I decided to look on the little chat as a time of useful observation which would help my understanding of him.

My understanding hasn't grown any better. But at least he no longer shakes me with all his angry strength. He doesn't touch me except on the blessedly rare occasions he wants sex and then it's in the most rudimentary way.

Ha! I used to call that endeavour 'making love'. Was love ever involved, on either side? To be honest, we had a need for each other, not love. I needed to escape from the rectory and acquire status. He needed an acolyte. An admirer, a dependent. I didn't understand the power balance for a long time.

Now the power balance is all too clear. He has the keys. They jangle from a chain around his waist.

Is he happy? I have no idea.

How long will this go on?

I have no idea.

There is sometimes a reward for the sex. Extra washing water. Once there was a rug to put down on the cement floor by the bed. Yesterday he gave me an apple.

"One of your five a day!" He roared with laughter.

His ability not to acknowledge our strange situation is simply extraordinary.

His sense of humour always has been weird.

From our earliest days of marriage, he was a puzzle to me. I couldn't believe that someone who needed his pyjamas neatly folded in a special way and tucked beneath his pillow could simultaneously discard on the floor used handkerchiefs, random socks and underpants. Alright, I thought, never mind: his mother must have done these little tidying up tasks without complaint. I will continue, also without complaint. So I did continue for years and years until – what shall I call it? The crisis.

Knives out. That's an expression, isn't it? I think it describes the stage in a meeting when amicable progress hits rough ground and it becomes obvious who disagrees with whom, who hates another, who is scheming for the top and who is for the chop. I never was in such a meeting in my life but I learnt about this sort of vicious backstabbing from Nicolas's little chats. After some years of listening, I boldly remarked that he never seemed to be the one at fault. Oh dear *me, I shouldn't have said such a thing!*

"You have no idea what I go through! You sit around at home, lady of leisure, doing your fingernails! I bend over backwards for the Board. Without me, the firm would sink, I can tell you. Why, just the other day," and off he'd go again.

I damped down my anger at the fingernails remark, and said not a thing in my own defence: how my days were full; how I was still working full-time as an office dogsbody to the firm of solicitors; how he should be pleased with my addition to his income. But no, it was as though I earned nothing. If, on a pay day, I bought steak, he'd fly off the handle. So I gave up buying steak. It wasn't worth the fury.

Given the trouble he had at meetings, it was amazing he clung on to his directorship so long. I thought it would be better when he retired. (Or was he pushed – I never knew). Our move to Torridon was to be a new beginning but he became even more difficult. He no longer had his fellow directors to quarrel with. He'd lost his authority, his power over employees. I filled in as target for his frustration and anger.

Somehow I survived. Until the crisis.

Don't ask me how long ago that was. I have no idea.

RACHEL 8

"Indian summer!" Rachel could hear her mother's voice in her head. After weeks of dull grey days, the sky had cleared and the sun was warm on her face as she set out on foot for the Middletons. Betty had promised to do her best to answer, over coffee, the various questions that Rachel had in mind. She wanted to tread the landscape that Elfrida had trod, perhaps even finding the site of the two domains mentioned in the poem. Both Betty and Stan's families had lived around there since the 16th century. They'd surely tell her the names of ancient settlements.

She would make a circle of her walk by returning by the bridle path that, according to the map, gave access to the Middletons' fields. Half way between the farm and the point where the path joined the road to the village, it passed the end of Torridon's land. She hoped there'd be a way of getting into the priory ruins without disturbing Clarkson.

"Oh, I don't think you'd be able to do that," said Betty looking alarmed. "He's been building up the boundary wall, Quite high. He says this is against the deer, getting into his garden. But what does he grow in his garden? Just bramble bushes!"

She went on to describe an incident when a couple of their sheep managed to get into Clarkson's garden despite the fortifications which Stan maintained along all the farm's boundaries, and particularly along the hedge-topped banks that bordered Torridon. "That was three years ago, come Michaelmas. What a state he got in! You'd think we'd ravaged his land." In her horror at the thought of Rachel climbing into Torridon's land she reverted to her Devonshire us's and ee's. *Ee'd think us'd* ...She told Rachel that the only way to see the ruins was to get Clarkson to give the say-so. And he'd never allow that in a month of Sundays.

Rachel thought otherwise. If a sheep had managed to get

over a bank, however thickly hedged on top, she could.

Later, standing crouched in a holly bush on the top of the boundary bank between the land belonging to the Middletons and the end of Clarkson's property, she revised her opinion. Her right arm was bleeding rather too profusely for comfort. Some of the hedgerow bushes had grown into small trees. Besides hawthorn and blackthorn, there were holly bushes and clumps of sycamore. She thought she'd chosen a likely point to make the attempt. First, she'd got down on hands and knees to crawl under the single strand of barbed wire into the ditch. Then she stood among the stinging nettles to consider the best way up the bank. She found enough footholds, grabbing at clumps of long grass and likely stones to clamber to the top where she'd thought there was a big enough gap in the vegetation. She was now in the midst of the hedge, prickly holly branches all around her. *All right for a sheep*, she thought. At the same time, she caught a glimpse of something moving among thickets of gorse.

No, not a sheep. It was a pale grey boulder. No, not a boulder. She realised she was looking down at the priory ruins, its ancient and crumbled stone walls visible here and there in the wilderness of gorse, brambles, nettles, old man's beard and who knows what.

She focused more carefully. What had caught her eye was not a boulder, nor a section of priory wall, but her neighbour. Nicolas Clarkson was roughly thirty yards away, doing something with a white bucket beside a gorse bush in vivid yellow bloom. His head was down. He hadn't spotted her. Nor had he heard her. She froze, rehearsing her options. If her neighbour was a normal man, she would call out a cheerful hello and he'd help her slither down the bank on the priory side. He would let her explore the ruins. There might be an invitation into the house, a cup of tea and a chat. They'd get to know each other better.

Or, if he was as weird as she thought he was, she would

very carefully retreat out of view.

    She very carefully retreated out of view.

ANGELA 9

Nicolas brought me a treat today. He allowed me to choose from the three which are usually on offer. I chose option two: half an hour with Nail Scissors. I'd had option one fairly recently; I didn't need to wash my hair with water for a while. Packets of dry shampoo do a good enough job. No-one's going to see me looking like a freak. The third option I dread receiving. Fry's Peppermint Cream disappears too quickly and I immediately yearn for more.

The worst thing about having treats – well, the second worst thing – is having Nicolas sitting in with me while I 'enjoy' the treat. I don't like being watched, particularly when it's the Shampoo treat. I have to deal with the jug of hot water, the mug, the shampoo and the bowl. It's so awkward. I never get a good rinse, there's never enough hot water, I feel ham-fisted, and all the time I have to be grateful to him, thanking him for the trouble. It is a kind of re-run of our past life together, magnified triplefold by the present circumstances. Hateful.

The first worst thing about a treat is that it's a reward for what he calls the performance of his conjugal rights: a perfunctory entry and exit that is painful, physically so because it's infrequent, and emotionally, because of the situation. At least when things were normal I could get through it by thinking of what I'd give myself afterwards: a slug of gin from the bottle I hid behind the bleach beneath the sink followed by a walk around the lanes, past the Middletons, along the bridle track, onto the village road and back to Torridon's track. I had a kind of freedom in those days. I don't think he knew about the gin, but he knew about the walk and allowed me this time on my own as a reward for succumbing to his need.

Nowadays there is no escape after the torture. Still, he allows me half an hour with the nail scissors despite what we both imagine is the danger. Sharp points!

Today he sat on the chair as I washed my hair. I had chosen Nails but, for some unfathomable reason, he brought hot water. I didn't say anything.

RACHEL 9

Rachel and Sally sat side by side on a boulder gazing at the view. At their backs lay the deep moat that circled the hill fort which they'd been exploring. At their feet, the ground fell away steeply towards the lane they'd driven along. Beyond, the countryside stretched away to the far horizon in a pattern of emerald green shapes threaded together by dark lines. Lit by the low sun, the trees in the hedgerows threw long shadows across the fields. In the centre of the view and winding down towards the south was the river, swollen by tributaries from higher in the hills. Pools of water lay on the river banks. It had rained for days but now – luckily for Sally's visit – it was a fine autumn day. The sun was warm on their faces. The two friends were silent, thinking their own thoughts.

Edna Johnson, in her notebook, had suggested that Elfrida had been born into a family who lived in a fortified farm called Bramflyte, which had been mentioned in the Domesday book. There was no Bramflyte marked on the map but Betty Middleton thought it must be near the iron age hill fort which had a similar name, Bramfleet Hill. If she was right, there could be some foundations still visible somewhere in or around the fort.

Rachel stared at the view, trying to imagine what it would have looked like in Elfrida's day. Did she too gaze down at the river from her family home? Or was this the place of the knight's domain, where she would have been brought as his wife had she not escaped to the priory? She examined her own feelings. Did she feel Elfrida was close? No. This was not a medieval landscape. The river, though? That would have run the same course, down through the valley towards the open sea. For a moment, she saw Elfrida tying back her long fair hair, gathering her dress above her ankles, stepping into the shallows. To cool off on a hot day? To collect a bucketful of water? She made her turn and look up at the hill with a small, calm smile.

A television programme she'd watched just a few days ago came to mind. She broke their companionable silence. "You see the river? The river that runs through our valley joins this one. You couldn't tell which water was which."

Sally glanced at Rachel with an expression of amused bafflement before turning back to the view.

She'd been all set to expand on her thought prompted by the programme she'd watched. The water analogy was apt, she thought, in relation to photons. She liked trying to get her mind around ideas, whatever the subject and however little she knew about it beforehand. The programme was about an experiment which took place on the highest ridge of a Californian mountain. Two vast telescopes directed light from two immensely far apart galaxies onto a small building, a kind of car park attendant's hut. This housed the subject of the experiment. Another hut housed a group of excited scientists. There were equations and diagrams galore which had the effect of bringing to Rachel's mind brief glimmers of understanding, only to whip the enlightenment away a moment later. In the past, she sometimes thought she had a tenuous grasp of the theory of relativity; she could visualise views from trains and changing perceptions. She knew from her own experience that things are influenced by other things in their immediate environment. She'd long since put down her own personality to the interaction between her parents' genes and the strange way they'd brought her up. It was another step altogether to comprehend that all this and the universe could be explained mathematically, with a tiny formula written in chalk on a blackboard. That was plainly ridiculous. Luckily, she'd now learnt that there was no longer any reason to understand Einstein's theory because it was out of date. The scientists on top of the mountain were about to put in its place Bell's theory. A diagram showed two groups of photons being affected by two beams of light from two separate galaxies. Arrows demonstrated how the photons in the groups mingled, jiggling from one diagrammatic test tube to another, paying no attention whatsoever to boundaries. One of the scientists, his eyes and teeth gleaming, told the camera that this proved that objects can be influenced outside the remits of space and time. This was the idea she wanted to explain to Sally with her river analogy. She was being influenced by Elfrida. Entanglement theory explained how the 13th century hermit had moved into her mind to become the object of her life and work.

It would have provided an interesting discussion. But it was clear that Sally had other things in mind, chief among them her plan to commission a greyhound weathervane. They were on their way to the forge, a visit arranged by Sally a week before.

"Great view, I agree," said Sally, getting to her feet. "But London for me. I'd go out of mind with boredom here." She held out a hand for Rachel. "Come on. Bob will be expecting us. It isn't far, is it?" She'd arranged the appointment without consulting Rachel.

Rachel disregarded the hand. She dreaded seeing Bob again as much as she wanted to. It was several weeks since he'd called in at the cottage. A few days after that visit, he'd phoned and suggested she join him for a walk; he regularly exercised several dogs for various owners; he mentioned the hill fort and Bramfleet woods. She struggled to find a way to refuse. On the surface it was an innocent invitation. He was just being friendly to her as a newcomer to the neighbourhood. There was no reason to suspect that he felt the same powerful sexual attraction that she'd experienced on their very first meeting. She'd have loved to join him on a walk with the dogs. But he belonged to Lucy. Looking down at the coppery-coloured woodland below, she seethed at her bad luck. There was a dreadful irony in the way that she'd extricated herself from one dead-end relationship only to fall for someone equally inappropriate. Was there something in her character that drew her to people who couldn't or wouldn't commit? It was true that she did like her independence but not to the extent of spending her life alone. She'd made the move to the country with the dim hope at the back of her mind that she would find her ideal man. She was certain she'd found him – *and he was out of bounds.*

It was almost as if Sally wanted her to become entangled – that word again – with another married man. For herself, she wanted to avoid any talk of Robert and his forge but that was hard without giving away how much she was attracted by him. She was not going to share her feelings with Sally for that would only make them more real. Instead, she'd talked incessantly of Elfrida and her sketching of Lucy as model, and she'd brought Sally to the possible location of Elfrida's family home. If she spun out their explorations long enough, Bob and the forge might have closed for the day.

"Have we time to have more of a hunt on the far side of the hill? I have a feeling that we're close to Elfrida."

"Really?" There was barely a question in her voice.

"I know you think I'm daft."

"A little, certainly."

"But you remember when we were the last visitors of the day to Glastonbury ruins?"

"You just saw a shadow."

"A shade, yes." Rachel recalled the sight of a young man in a feather-plumed hat, approaching her through an archway. In mock, ghostly tones, she recited, *"I saw a man upon the stair. I looked again. He wasn't there. He wasn't there again today. I wish that man would go away."*

""Don't scare me, Ray. You know I can't take it!"

Rachel, laughing, got to her feet. "Elfrida trod this ground, without a doubt."

She wasn't as convinced as she sounded. However, to delay the visit to the forge, she persuaded Sally to continue the search for any sign that there had once been a manor of some importance in the area of the hill fort. The only trace of human habitation they found, past or present, was a collapsed and abandoned tent.

ANGELA 10

Time ceases to exist when you live underground without natural light. Is this the worst part of it, I wonder? When no lines are drawn between day and night, or one day and the next, it's easy to go mad. I sometimes wonder if that would be the route to take; to become so deranged that he'd be forced to let me go. But no, he couldn't do that. How would he explain the sudden re-appearance of a wife after so long? Not all the questions could be answered by madness. He'd be more likely to kill me. And I know he won't do that. I'm his addiction. To have me totally in his power is the inevitable outcome of what started when he married me. I'm his life blood. Like cocaine or alcohol. Kept in a never-ending supply under his workshop. Well, that must be where I am. He never takes very long to fetch whatever he's forgotten to bring with him.

I tested this in the early days. I managed to draw blood with my most precious possession – the sharp stone I found almost at once and hid in a crevice in the rock wall. When he brought my meal, I made sure blood was welling from my wrist. He rushed away to fetch his first aid kit which lives in the bathroom cabinet. I'd counted to 450 by the time he returned; long enough, I reckoned, to go back to Torridon and return to his workshop. Before the knife crisis, he'd spent months excavating a pit behind his workshop, creating a heat exchange system or so he said. I'm under his workshop, I'm sure of it.

It was a step forward being able to imagine my precise location, and I was pleased with my trick on Nicolas. A morale boost. He has a horror of blood. When we first married, this was one of the many things that took me by surprise. In the rectory we never covered up a wound. Let it see the fresh air, said my mother. Plasters were things in other people's bathroom cabinets; never in ours. When on honeymoon I slipped in Boscastle harbour – the tide was out, I was looking for crabs in the rock pools – Nicolas all but fainted. I am afraid I laughed at the sight of him, and that made him furious. So there I was with blood running down my leg, laughing happily, and there was my husband collapsed on a rock, holding his hands over his eyes. A family group not far away was watching with great interest at this strange human drama. I held a tissue against the cut and hobbled back to the hotel on my own to wash it clean. I realised then that I would probably never get sympathetic help from Nicolas. It would be best not to need it.

RACHEL 10

They were longer than they'd thought they'd be at Bramfleet fort and, on arrival at the forge, they found Bob in the process of locking up. Rachel wished they'd been a moment later. Bob would have left; there would have been no point in following him, disturbing Lucy and the children when they were probably about to have a meal. She would have been saved from the temptation of – not exactly flirting with him, but of relaxing her control. She'd learnt years ago that she could attract sexual attention or deflect it, purely through her own attitude. It was like a switch, either on or off. She likened the two states to a car's headlights; you either have them on full beam or dipped.

It was difficult to stay dipped with Rob. She tried not to respond to his smiles and enthusiasm as he ushered them into the forge, brushing aside their apologies. She was intensely aware of his physical presence. With Sally ahead of her, she was able to notice more about him today than on their previous two meetings. His height, for a start. To be with a man taller than herself was always welcome. He was not overweight but he did have remarkably wide shoulders and a broad chest. His hair grew in tight curls. She imagined winding a curl around her finger before letting it spring loose. Like making curls in Christmas parcel ribbon. His eyes, hazel brown, or were they green, regarded her with a watchful, amused expression. He emanated energy and strength. The thought came to her that he could forge iron without the need of a fire. But of course she wouldn't share such a thought, however apt it was. Stay aloof, she told herself. Keep cool.

She hung back, letting Sally take the lead. The first surprise was that there was no evidence of a fire at all. She'd imagined the forge as she would draw it for a children's book: Bob the Blacksmith, in a long, heavy, leather apron, hammering at a red hot iron bar, sparks flying, metal hissing, a blazing, coal furnace in the background. But no, she could see nothing like that. It was hard to make out anything at all. She peered into the darkness of a low-ceilinged workshop, stacked high with unidentifiable grey and black objects sticking out at all angles. A narrow alleyway between towering stacks led into the gloom. If she'd known nothing about Bob, she'd assume he ran a junkyard. Sally was already expressing her own surprise. "Where's the fire?" she asked.

Bob came to halt by a workbench, its surface piled high with hefty-looking equipment. "Oh. You thought --? Sorry to disappoint. We're all electric these days."

He launched into an excited description of modern methods and his preference for decorative ironwork over shoeing horses, with Sally listening avidly at this elbow. He showed her a folder of photographs of his work while Rachel stayed near the open doorway. Every so often Bob looked in her direction, wanting to include her. She avoided his glance by paying close attention to the many and various things piled on all available surfaces and hanging from hooks on the dark walls, their purposes a mystery although she did recognise an anglegrinder with its heavy electrical lead wound around its handle. Then there was a jumble of black shapes that on closer inspection turned out to be a fire screen, a grate, a candelabra and a bouquet of iron rosebuds in a vase. All kinds of things could be forged with iron. People came here for courses, she'd been told by Lucy. If only Bob didn't have this disastrous effect on her, if only he didn't belong to Lucy, she'd take one of his courses. She imagined designing and making a house sign for Priory Cottage. She saw it hanging at the entrance to the track: Priory Cottage, a black silhouette of – of – Elfrida herself? A simple black outline, sideview.

Sally's voice broke into her thoughts. "Must it be a greyhound? Bob's saying that he did a beautiful Weimaraner recently."

"Come and have a look," said Bob. "This is for you, after

all."

She joined them at the workbench, making sure that Sally was between her and Bob. She hoped her voice would sound firm. "I'm not sure that a Weimaraner would be right. Not English. And too big for Elfrida who I imagine was small and slight."

Bob flicked through the folder. "A medieval English hound. Hmm."

If she'd lain a hand on his chest, she'd have felt his voice rumble. She dismissed the thought. "A whippet?" she suggested. "Descended from greyhounds, I think, and generally smaller and more delicate?"

"Delicate? I'll have to make it robust. Weather vanes take a lot of weather." He went on to talk of the practicalities.

Rachel tried to concentrate on what he was saying.

"You've got to get things right in the first place. Once up, it should stay there without attention. I give my vanes a ridiculous number of layers of high quality black paint. You can't just nip up onto the roof and give the model a fresh coat every so often. Same goes for all the invisible bits. The bearings in the shaft for instance. You can't have a vane stuck, pointing in the same direction all the time. It must swing easily with the wind, yet be strong enough to withstand gales."

Rachel imagined a whirling weathervane creaking over her head. "Can a vane go on a thatched roof? We should have asked that before."

"I did ask that!" Sally sounded hurt.

It was Sally who'd arranged this appointment with Bob; they'd talked on the phone, probably at length. At the pottery party, it was Sally who had been sitting on the sofa next to Bob. Although Bob was not a conventionally good-looking man, it occurred to her that Sally might have the same response to him as she had. And Sally might not worry unduly about Lucy. Way back in the London past, it was she who had encouraged Rachel's involvement with Malcolm, paying no attention at all to his married status. "It's one of those open marriages," she had assured Rachel at the time. No – if Sally found Bob desirable, she wouldn't hold back. She'd pursue him in her usual predatory fashion.

The realisation put Rachel on her guard.

"Is this the sort of thing you had in mind?" asked Bob holding the folder open for Sally at a photograph of an ironwork fox silhouetted within a wreath of ivy.

Before Sally could express an opinion, Rachel answered quickly. "Mm, that's attractive. Intricate work. But is it robust enough?"

"Certainly. Nothing goes out of this workshop that isn't robust."

She felt rebuked. She hadn't intended to question the standard of his work. "Oh, I didn't mean," she began and then hesitated. If she retracted or apologised, it would make more of the interchange than it merited. She sensed that this was one of those moments that go by at speed but have lasting significance. Without being able to work out what was happening between them, she knew she must steer quickly away from her unintended slur on his ability. "Actually, I'm rather thinking," she began slowly, feeling her way, "that it might be better to have a house sign instead of a weathervane." Sally might be paying, but the present was for her. "What about Priory Cottage in medieval script?" She could visualise it as soon as she said it.

Her two listeners were clearly taken aback. She went on. "I'm not sure about the juxtaposition of materials." She shouldn't have used such a cumbersome word. "Thatch and iron. So different, so close together. What do you think?"

"I thought it would be attached to the chimney pot at the far end of the cottage roof?" put in Sally. "The chimney pot is brick, isn't it?"

Bob was also speaking. "No reason why you can't have a weathervane on a thatch roof." He was looking at her with an expression she couldn't fathom. If she were to draw his face, she'd have trouble with the two lines that bracketed his wide mouth; their depth and angle changed all the time. His eyes, too. She couldn't possibly catch their hazel-green translucence. The colour of a dark mossy rock beneath a layer of river water. He was still regarding her.

She was glad when Sally broke the silence that was stretching out between them. She didn't like losing her weathervane idea. "I can't think where you'd put a house sign. In the car park? Who would see it?"

"No, in the lane. At the entrance to the track. Nicolas has put a huge Torridon sign there. It seems he's making some sort of point. I'd like to answer him. *I'm here too!*"

It didn't take her long to persuade Sally and Bob that a house sign must replace the weathervane. Bob found a block of paper and a pencil and began to rough out a design. Rachel watched the way his hand moved over the paper. He was a good and confident draughtsman, she was glad to see. He encouraged her to show him what she had in mind. The paper became the ground on which they met, their pencils sharing murmured ideas: *Could go like this? Or like this? What about that?* It was only when they had agreed on a design that she realised how much she'd enjoyed the experience of sharing. Perhaps he would help with her Elfrida book? It would be such a *holiday* to share all the decision-making. As soon as the thought struck her, she banished it. For the past five minutes, she'd completely forgotten her vow to hold back. Now Sally had turned the discussion towards prices. She suggested that Rachel should absent herself. "I don't want you knowing how much or how little I'm spending on you. Why don't you pop in next door? I'm sure Lucy would like to see you."

Rachel was glad to leave the dark workshop which was overfull, not just of things but of conflicting emotions. Whatever had just happened would need time for reflection. For the moment she was glad to be outside, on her own, in the dark, chill air. She went slowly through the workshop's yard which was as full of unnameable objects as the forge itself had been. A low and straggly hedge divided the yard from the front garden of the house. The door was ajar. She went inside and called but there was no answer. Sounds came from upstairs. Against a background of the baby's wails, she could hear splashing water and joyful squeals: bathtime excitement. She went up and found Lucy, sitting on a stool beside the bath, her ringletted hair caught up in a knot on top of her head, a towel on her lap. The two little girls, with similar blonde and curly top-knots, were in the bath, pink-cheeked and round-eyed, suddenly silent. They regarded Rachel as though she'd dropped from the sky.

"Oh great!" Lucy jumped up from the stool, handing the towel to Rachel. "I have to feed the baby. You've come just at the right moment."

Rachel apologised for keeping Bob so late in the forge.

"I'm sure he didn't mind a bit."

"But I bet you could do with his help at this time of day."

"Why on earth would he help?"

Rachel was surprised that Bob and Lucy had such an old-fashioned attitude to a father's role in the home. She assumed that all parents shared end-of-day family time and tasks. But maybe that was a London view. Before she could query this, Lucy had left the bathroom and the two girls were clamouring for attention.

"Thope my back! Thope my back!"

Nervously – this was a first - she soaped their bird-like rib cages and knobbly spines. What would their father's body be like? Banish the thought.

ANGELA 11

Yesterday, Nicolas brought me the remains of a Chicken Korma and it's had a very bad effect. I've told him many times that curries don't suit me. Still, it's his funeral. He has to empty my slops, so serve him right.

I sometimes think that, in a way, he's my prisoner, rather than I'm his. He has to look after me, if he wants to keep me alive. Which he obviously does. So I must be constantly in his mind. I can imagine him at breakfast making a list of things to do. He used to do this daily without fail. There's no reason why he hasn't continued. He probably has two columns on his list, one for him and the house, one for me and my needs.

My needs must feature far more frequently than ever they did when I sat beside him in the kitchen. What a chore he's given himself!

I like the thought.

Last night – I expect it was another effect of the curry – I was remembering the time when we invited the Johnsons in to supper with us. To invite people in was a rare event, so rare that we both got in a state about it sometime before the actual day. I was nervous about the cooking; Nicolas kept agonising over the question of drink. What should he get in? Were they wine drinkers? Gin and tonic for starters? Sherry perhaps? Or would we go straight in with white, chilled, before red with the meal? Was Lionel Johnson a beer man? Did Ruth drink? He rather thought she didn't. In which case what soft drink should we provide? What would the meal consist of? Nicolas wanted to get a leg of lamb from the Middletons. They were sure to have one of their own in their freezer. I wanted to do a chicken casserole, something I was confident of managing. It would save me the awful business of a roast, getting lots of different things ready at the right time: roast potatoes, whatever veg I'd serve. Gravy. Mint sauce. A nightmare.

Nicolas brought a large leg of lamb back from the Middletons the day before the occasion. Chicken casserole was off the menu.

Exactly as I dreaded and expected.

We didn't sleep too well and there was something companion-like about the restlessness the looming occasion caused. It took me years to understand that my masterful, competent husband could actually be nervous.

*I've had lots of time to go over this in my mind. We began our married life on the basis of mutual misapprehension. In the early days, I thought Nicolas was right about everything. He knew about things. I didn't. I admired the way he managed our finances, opened and shut doors for me, handled all our paperwork, talked forcefully and at length to business associates on the phone. I didn't realise it was an act, covering up insecurity. He was like one of those animals which puff themselves up to twice their size, for fear of being small and beaten. Inside, he **was** small and beaten. Gradually, I learnt how he and his mother had been constantly manipulated and browbeaten by his father. This was something I remembered when he behaved in similar fashion towards me. I let him be the big man out of the compassion for the child he tried to hide. My rectory upbringing made me bend over backwards to make his life easy. See God in everyone, preached my father from the pulpit. I prayed -* Gentle Jesus, meek and mild, look upon a little child *– kneeling on cold lino at my bedside.*

Meek and mild, I was a gift for Nicolas, I see that now, so long as I carried on as I did at the start of our marriage. But as the years went by, I occasionally dared to express my own opinions. He hated that. He needed me to be small and silent. In that way, he didn't need to puff himself up to be bigger. He was bigger. I thought so. He thought so. I can hear his constantly angry voice attacking me. "Why the blazes can't you sharpen the carving knife before I need to use it?"

"Sorry."

"Why the hell can't you buy decent bread?"

"Sorry."

"Why the fuck can't you – ?"

"Sorry."

This was my technique for a quiet life. As far as possible I avoided upsetting him. If I could foresee a possible cause of upset, I could take pre-emptive action. I made sure his walking shoes were always clean. I made coffee in the "right" way. I answered the phone as he liked me to answer it. Phone number first, then "Angela Clarkson speaking." This had to be immediately followed by, "May I give my husband a message?" This was puzzling for the few people who wanted to speak to me, rather than Nicolas. But never mind, it had to be done this way or all hell broke loose. Things got thrown across rooms, not just phones.

If, woe betide, something unforeseen happened to cause an outburst, then the only course of action was immediate apology. Humble pie. No explanations. No justifications. Just "Sorry!" As time went by, these unforeseen incidents became more frequent. It was as though he needed an excuse to erupt. A whale comes to the surface to blow. Nicolas needed regular blow-outs. If he hadn't been provided with an excuse for a while, he created a reason from nothing at all. The sudden eruption would floor me. Not only was it a shock out of the blue, its inexplicable cause made it harder.

I used to take myself away. When we lived in Fulham, I would go to the cinema. I found a film, any film, soothing. Of course, on my return I had to pay for the time out. Recriminations, resentment, a slow burn over days, this kind of pay-back was easier to manage than the eruptions; because I felt he was justified. I'd gone to the cinema on my own, seen a film on my own. I'd chosen flight to fight. I never fought. Why would I? I'm not an idiot. Until, as I keep reminding myself, the knife incident. But despite this hell, I don't regret it. Not really.

Way back, when he had the London office, he had staff to bother about, bark at, be furious with. They obeyed his commands. I had a few friends, chief among them my ex flat mates, who would listen open-mouthed to my reports of his behaviour. But I never wanted to be disloyal to Nicolas and anything I related, I did so lightly, for their amused horror rather than their serious concern. I certainly didn't give anything away to my parents while they were still alive. They would have been upset to think that our marriage was anything other than happy.

When we moved to Torridon, I had the foolish idea that life with Nicolas would be easier. No such luck; it was far worse. At Torridon, it was only me in the firing line. No office staff to take the brunt. No friends for me to wail to. I found it hard to make friends in the countryside. I felt like a fish out of water. Only our neighbour, Ruth Johnson, seemed to understand what was going on. She sometimes knocked on the door and offered me a lift into town, or a coffee and a chat at Priory Cottage. I usually turned her away, finding one excuse or another. To accept would be letting the side down. Nicolas hated me going out on my own, so I rarely did. "Why's she offering you a lift? We've got a perfectly good car of our own." "Coffee and a chat? Why's she wanting you to go in for a coffee and a chat? Haven't we got coffee? Don't we chat?" The answer yes only applied to the coffee. His chat was all about his own plans, thoughts and feelings, never about mine. I slowly realised that I only existed as a segment of his own being, not as a separate entity. (Talk about Adam's rib!). This realisation should have helped. It didn't. It drove me to dangerous action, to cut myself free.

Our neighbours, the Johnsons, were a direct contrast to us. I've never seen a couple so kind to each other, so happy with their life together. I watched them with astonishment during our roast lamb meal. They didn't get at each other in any way. And there was nothing in the slightest bit forced or fake about them.

They were what you might call a sweet old couple but that sounds patronising. They both could make quite sharp, but never malicious, remarks. Nicolas wanted me to give them the works: table mats on the polished mahogany, best Waterford glass and Georgian silver cutlery (wedding present from my grandmother, still alive at the time). White linen napkins with my mother's initials embroidered in white in the corner (and never ever used in the rectory, so they smelt of the drawer in the oak chest they were kept in for half a century: moth balls' naphtheline mixed with stale and musty lavender). The Johnsons, sitting opposite each other, made me think of a pair of doves, nodding, pecking and coooing in unison. To look at them, you might think Lionel and Ruth were brother and sister, even twins. Their faces had aged in the same way. They were perhaps in their early 80s, both with wispy, white hair over pink scalps. They, like me, were on the short side; in fact, our heads at the table were on a level while Nicolas, sitting straight-backed at the head of the table, looked down on us.

"How very kind of you to go to all this trouble," said Ruth, unfolding her napkin and smoothing it neatly over her lap. She was wearing an emerald green tunic kind of thing over trousers which looked like a matching pair to Lionel's grey flannels. He wore a red check shirt under a dark grey V-necked sweater. Nicolas was in his navy-blue suit with a white shirt and his Cricket Club tie. I knew I shouldn't have worn the dress that Nicolas had put out for me. It was his favourite and he'd chosen it himself one Christmas. Its shoulders had been put out of shape by its hanger and never recovered no matter how hard and often I worked at them with the iron. He couldn't believe such a good dress had been reduced so much in the sale. He had to tell me that. The excellence of the price and the quality of the material overrode a natural reluctance to admit it was a sale bargain. On every occasion I wore that dress, it felt like a bad mistake. I could have stayed in my jeans, and the Johnsons wouldn't have minded one way or another. Most probably, they wouldn't have even noticed.

"I so rarely bother with a roast," went on Ruth.

"No trouble at all," said Nicolas.

"This is a real treat," said Lionel.

"We used to give our students a Sunday roast every now again. But that was – how long ago now, love?"

"Twenty years, it must be!"

"Twenty! Just think."

The Johnsons, we now learnt, had run a language school in Exeter for foreign students wanting to improve their English for university courses. They also trained people to teach English to foreigners; this, they explained with painstaking detail, was known by the initials TEFL, standing for Teaching English as a Foreign Language. They'd clearly loved the work. Ruth, apparently, was the better linguist and teacher, while Lionel ran the place and looked after the foreign students. Pastoral Care, he called it. I felt I could benefit from the same kind of patient attention they obviously gave their students. He had trained as a counsellor and carried on a practice in Exeter while running the school.

"I don't suppose you still work as a counsellor, do you?" I asked. "Oh dear, am I being ageist?"

Ruth, chewing on a piece of meat – it was tough, I know, I'd over or under cooked it, who knows which - waved her hand sideways in my direction as though cancelling out my gaffe.

Nicolas said, "I do apologise for my wife. She doesn't think before she speaks."

"No need to apologise!" exclaimed both Johnsons at the same time in the same way.

I felt the blood had flooded to my face. It would have been perfectly okay if Nicolas had just stayed silent.

His remark was completely unjust. I never spoke, at least in his company, unless I'd thought out very carefully its likely effect on him.

And now I hardly ever speak at all. When I do, my voice comes out as a low croak.

"Speak up, for god's sake!" says Nicolas nowadays.

He's growing deaf. Or rather, deafer than ever

I was never sure whether it was deafness that stopped him hearing me. Even in the early years of our marriage, he wouldn't respond to something I said. I had to repeat it several times before I knew he'd heard it. Whether this was due to chronic deafness or – and this I think it much more likely – he simply disregarded me. He didn't have to hear what his wife was thinking any more than he had to take the view of a neighbour into account or, for that matter, any inanimate object. He paid more attention to his car's communications, warning lights, beeping, than mine.

The only time when he really listened to someone else's views was when he needed something from them – in business or in his private life. That was why I was surprised by his attitude towards the Johnsons, which was evident during that evening we had them to a meal. What was it that he wanted from them? I cannot imagine. They were such a gentle, undemanding couple. How they managed to handle their students, I don't know. But Nicolas kowtowed to them. I reckon his manner towards Lionel and Ruth had something to do with the priory ruins at the bottom of our garden.

He'd bought Torridon so that he could boast about having medieval ruins in his garden. I know he thought it was positively baronial to possess a priory, however long it had been in ruins. It wasn't as though he was going to let anyone else see them. He was neurotic about anyone straying onto his land. I don't say "our" land because it didn't feel like mine in any way, although my name was – still is, I wonder? – on the deeds and my family money helped buy the place.

At the time of our arrival in the neighbourhood, the Johnsons were getting together a group of people with the aim of opening the ruins to the public. The Mitchells, the previous owners of Torridon, had been thinking of this as supplementary income. In the end they were frightened off by all the regulations involved and the amount of restoration needed to make it viable. An easier way to boost their finances was to sell Torridon. The Johnsons, on the other hand, were still keen and probably hoped that we would be, too.

While I was making coffee after the meal, Nicolas handed Lionel the box file of Torridon papers left behind by the Mitchells. I overheard the exchange. I remember thinking: he's being like an English explorer, pacifying the natives with beads.

Lionel's voice "But this is marvellous!"

Ruth: "Amazing!"

Lionel: "Good Lord! Ruth, look at this!"

Ruth: "What is it?"

Lionel: "The ballad! The Reverend Eliot McElligott's Elfrida poem is here. Just wonderful. And maps. Clive Mitchel was going to hand all this over for the project."

Ruth: "He forgot. We didn't like to ask."

Lionel: "So it would be wonderful if we might borrow it for a while?"

Ruth: "For PRP."

Lionel: "The Priory Restoration Project."

Ruth: "You do intend to carry on with the Mitchells' plan?"

Lionel: "They said you would."

Nicolas: "They said I would?"

I could hear the danger signals. I hurried to get the coffee tray ready to take in. Pouring oil on troubled waters was what I did all the time.

Nicolas:. "They may have said as much to you but I have no intention whatsoever of becoming a public trampling ground."

Ruth: "Trampling ground! It wouldn't be at all like that!"

Lionel, soothingly: "Didn't the Mitchells describe it to you? Once we've cut back all the vegetation and propped up the ..."

Ruth: "The walls."

Lionel: "Made the ground safe and so forth, we will allow people in."

Ruth: "Just on Sundays. We thought £5 a head."

Nicolas: "I don't care what you thought you'd charge. I'm not having people tramping all over my property."

Trampling or tramping. In the build-up to an explosion he often had trouble getting words out.

Me: "Now who was it who wanted black coffee?"

Nicolas, calming down: "You are welcome to keep the box so long as we have no more talk about a project on My Land." *The capital letters were audible.*

RACHEL 11

It was a bright, dry December morning, two weeks before Christmas. Rachel was throwing forkfuls of hedge cuttings onto a bonfire from a growing pile fed by Oliver. He was working on the boundary hedge between the cottage and Torridon. He was whistling. Rachel was relieved to see him cheerful for the first time that autumn. Matt, apparently, had made the decision to leave his wife. He had moved in again. "At least," said Oliver, "for the time being." He was being realistic. "I'm not going to assume anything. Just enjoy the moment." They were going to Morocco for Christmas.

That left Rachel in limbo. She had thought Oliver would come to her, and they'd re-create, even in rather a minimal way, their childhood Christmases.. She had put aside some foliage from the hedge cuttings in order to make a wreath for the front door. She'd always made Christmas wreaths and had hung a series on a number of front doors, from Wimbledon, to Streatham, to Battersea and now for the Priory Cottage door. But did she any longer feel like going to the trouble? Just for herself?

Oliver's whistling was getting on her nerves. It wasn't continuous. It alternated with the chainsaw's racket and stopped altogether as he climbed up and down the newly exposed bank. He had cleared much of the scrub at the margin between the garden and the bank and was working his way slowly along the hawthorn, blackthorn, holly, ash and sycamore that grew thickly on top. Rachel was aware that, as Oliver had grown more cheerful, she had grown more depressed. She was beginning to feel she had made a severe mistake in giving up her London life. Her relationship with Malcolm had after all been ideal. She had none of the bothers of domesticity with him. With her work on Walter, she had no money worries. It had all been easy and pleasurable – or so it now seemed. She knew she was blanking out the dark side of her London life – the lack of a shared future, the way she had to take second place to Malcolm's wife, who could insist on his company at a weekend without notice. She should remember that it hadn't been perfect.

And Malcolm would never have taken a decision like Matt's. From the start, he'd made it plain that he'd never leave his wife.

"For god's sake, Oliver, can't you at least whistle in tune?"

He'd added another huge load of cuttings to the pile. She gave the fire another forkful. The flames crackled higher. She'd even lost her usual pleasure in a bonfire.

Now she was to be on her own at Christmas. None of the people she had got to know in the neighbourhood would ask her to join them. That's an invitation you only give to old friends. She was viewed as a newcomer and would be, she knew, for years and years. Only Lucy and Rob were the sort of people who might invite her – but she'd vowed not to let her mind stray in that direction.

She'd ring Sally and see what her plans were for Christmas. She could go and stay with Sally in Battersea. She would not be downhearted. She would not become a bitter old maid.

Oliver had returned to her side. He had a hand on her arm and was mouthing something at her.

"What?" she asked irritably.

He jerked his head towards the bank. "He's appeared." His mouth formed the words. "He's making for his workshop."

Heads bent, they froze in attitudes of bonfire-feeding. A moment passed. The bonfire's flames licked at the holly leaves, making a satisfying crackle.

Then they heard Nicolas's sharp voice. "Hey there!" He was standing on top of the bank, peering over the trimmed part of the hedge.

Rachel felt caught out, like a schoolgirl about to be punished for running in the corridor. She jabbed her pitch fork into the ground and went over to the bank.

Nicolas was shouting something about scrub. She couldn't make it out. She went to the foot of the bank.

"Oh hello, Nicholas," she said in as ordinary way as she could summon. "Isn't it a lovely day." She looked up at him, summoning all her powers to charm. She noticed the deep lines carved on his brow and around his mouth: a comic book artist's indication of anger.

"I remember telling you this the last time you began to attack my hedge." His tone was cold, precise and reasonable.

"I'm sorry. What did you tell me?"

"The importance of scrub!"

Scrub? What was he on about? How was she going to respond? What had he said before? It must be something to do with cutting back the hedge, but surely it wasn't altogether his hedge? She should have checked this. She looked to Oliver for help but he wasn't beside her. The rotter had busied himself with the bonfire.

"Oh, so sorry. I must have misunderstood," she said, ashamed at her cowardice. Why did she feel she couldn't stand up to her neighbour? She, who could get her own way with editors and art departments.

"Borderline scrub is essential for the whole cycle of nature. It's one of the richest natural habitats on Planet Earth."

Over lunch, Rachel relayed the conversation – a shortened version – to Oliver. She wished she could convey the strained tone of Nicolas's voice, the tic jumping in the corner of one glittering eye.

"I'm sure it all made absolute sense, but his manner makes one think he's stark, staring mad. I really don't understand him. He was clutching a tin of baked beans. What on earth was he doing with a tin of baked beans? On his way to his workshop?"

"Perhaps he gets peckish of a morning."

"And he had more tins stuffed into the pockets of his Barbour!"

They laughed in unison. Rachel wished she saw more of her brother. They'd always shared the same horrified amusement at the idiosyncracies displayed by their parents' academic friends, mostly historians.

"Do you know what he does in his workshop?" asked Oliver.

"Well, he's an antique dealer. Lucy tells me that he goes to auctions all over the place. His barn – you know, at the end of the track before the car park? – that's full of things he's bought and will restore one day. That's what he does in his workshop, apparently. Restoration. Not just furniture but big, old oil paintings, too. Valuable pieces, Lucy thinks. The odd thing is: the barn doesn't have doors that can be locked. It backs onto the buildings to the side of the house. The stables of the house in its heyday, I guess. Probably stuffed with more auction bargains and with doors that can be locked. But he keeps his ride-on mower and its tow truck at the back of the open barn as well as his Navara."

"The way he is with his precious hedges you'd think he'd have everything he owns under lock and key."

"He probably thinks he can keep people out just by shouting at them."

"He shouted at me when I first visited, and if I wasn't your brother, I think I would have fled!"

"In the six months I've been here I've only noticed one visitor, and that was Stan Middleton on his tractor."

Oliver produced his favourite saying, "None so queer as folks."

ANGELA 12

Nicolas has had his beard trimmed. He can't have done it himself, it looks too neat for that. It's also more severely trimmed than usual. It makes him look younger. The thought comes to me: could he be seeing another woman? A younger woman? And why not? In the world he inhabits, he's a single man. There are no two ways about that. I can see him leaning on a desk being charming to someone like me, a young naïve girl like I was when he leant on my desk and asked me out.

The possibility has been going around my head for hours. I can't dislodge it.

Why should I worry if Nicolas is pursuing a young woman? I should be glad he's got an interest beyond his obsession with me, keeping me alive.

Ah. That's why I should be worried. If he is after a young woman, then he would definitely want to make me totally disappear. He wouldn't want to be trotting between house and workshop with food and water, watched by a lovely young woman who attends to his every need.

If there really is a young woman in his life, then my days are numbered. Would I be glad?

Sometimes I long for a final exit. Especially on the days when I can't stop weeping. The cold, damp and dark get to me. If I was sane, I should welcome his interest in someone else.

On the other hand, I do not want to die. I still hope for rescue, even after all this time. The life force is very strong. I know that.

I could give up eating and drinking. He couldn't make me eat, unless he adopted the methods of force-feeding. But I don't think he would resort to that. He has his own standards of conduct.

People do die if they don't take in food and water for days. I'm not sure how long it takes. There's a certain number of days you can last without food and a shorter length of time you can last without water. In my Torridon life, I'd google that for an answer. But I'm not, which is why I want to google the question. There's irony for you.

I don't think I'm strong-minded enough to follow this course. My sharp stone is my ally. A little pain helps me survive.

RACHEL 12

It was strange to be back in Battersea. Rachel had been looking forward eagerly to spending Christmas with Sally. Now she was here, she longed to be home in Priory Cottage. Within the flat, despite the double glazing, she felt hammered by the continuous blast of traffic. Outside, she hated having to breathe in diesel and petrol fumes. Another shock was the way everyone walked and talked at high speed, as though disastrously late for their next appointment. She realised how used she'd become to fresh air, long views, empty lanes, slow conversations, and having all the time in the world; that is, as far as her own life was concerned.

"Them bleddy folks, us'd be bleddy mazed," she told Sally, in poor imitation of Stan Middleton. In her normal voice she continued, "Even walking along a pavement, I feel I'm going to be mown down."

Sally laughed. "More likely, people jump out of your way. Even buses take a detour!"

Rachel, joining in the laughter, had always been surprised to hear Sally's view of her. She wanted it to be a fair picture but she never believed it was accurate. All the same, she was glad to be such a formidable character, if only in Sally's eyes.

But she had changed and Sally didn't see it. They no longer knew each other in the way they had done when they were neighbours. For years, they'd shared so much. Sally had been the first to buy the Battersea flat. Then she'd encouraged Rachel to go for the next one that came up for sale in the same block, a converted terrace of Edwardian houses. The prices were reasonable at the time and the leases were long. Rachel's semi-basement flat was smaller than Sally's but it did include a garden room which she'd used as her studio. It was two minutes from the park and an easy walk over the river to Chelsea. In fact, it pleased their shared art school background to consider it to be not Battersea at all, but the southern boundary of Chelsea.

This attitude was shared by other residents, particularly by the couple who lived in the top floor flat: Robin Stevens, a well-known journalist, and Moira, who'd been on the fringe of the group of artists known as the YBAs. Moira was no longer young but she was still British and an artist; that is, if you could call her work Art, which Rachel was reluctant to do. In her view, conceptual art should have stopped with Marcel Duchamp's loo. Still, the Stevens held good Boxing Day parties and she and Sally had always been invited. They were going again this year. Rachel wasn't at all sure she wanted to, but Sally was keen.

"There'll be the usual crowd and the usual surprises," said Sally as she poured two glasses of milk. "To line our stomachs," she added.

The surprise Rachel dreaded was the appearance of Malcolm. But he never had been at the Boxing Day party. He belonged to a different circle. Besides, he was unlikely to break his rule of being with his wife and family over Christmas and New Year.

"Moira will be in a state of high excitement. She's been commissioned to do the arrival of spring for the forecourt of a German bank. In Berlin."

"Good for her," said Rachel.

She had mixed feelings about the Stevens. Robin's conversation she found hard to follow. He assumed she knew and understood very much more about economics than she really did. This was on the grounds that one Boxing Day she'd quoted something she'd read recently about quantitative easing. Robin mistakenly assumed the opinion came straight from her brain. He saw it as a green light to expand at length on whatever was intriguing him in the financial world at the time. As for Moira, Rachel guessed she looked down on Walter the Warthog's mass market success. Now that Rachel had put Walter away in mothballs and retired to the country, Moira's attitude might have become even more dismissive. Sally was safe from such unease.

She'd adapted to the changing demands of publishers and was getting lots of commissions for the kind of artwork that could only be done on computer. Moira approved – according to Sally.

"She wants me to teach her how to use the app I work with."

"Does she now."

"Shall I wear my hair up or down?"

"Up."

Sally snatched a clump of hair and held it on top of her head, while checking her reflection in a small mirror tacked to the kitchen wall. She tilted her head to one side and regarded the effect.

"No. Down," said Rachel.

"Sure?"

"No. Not sure. Whatever makes you happy."

"*Nothing* about my hair makes me happy."

Sally should be pleased with her sleek, black hair that always fell neatly into place, unlike her own which had a will of its own. Is anyone ever satisfied, she wondered. Her mind turned to the golden ringlets of Elfrida, and from there to the cascade of blonde waves belonging to Lucy, her living model. Lucy longed for hair like Sally's. Her thoughts slid from Lucy to Robert. She saw him in his forge, roughing out a house sign for her. She felt queasy. If only she could seal off one thought from another, but they all came tumbling in together: Elfrida, Lucy, Robert.

"Are you okay?" asked Sally in alarm. "You look like you've seen a ghost. Sit down for a second?"

Rachel sat down. She ought to eat something before the party to settle her stomach, not just drink milk.

The Stevens' flat was formed from the original attics of three of the terraced houses, now knocked into one. A wall of glass onto a long balcony acted like a magnet for the guests.

Everyone wanted to place and name what they could make out from the myriad lights pricking bright holes in the dark shapes of buildings under the bruised sky. There were many disagreements. Rachel listened at the edge of a group of four. She knew exactly what could be seen but she would not take part. She didn't want to appear a know-all, especially as she could no longer claim any part of the view.

"No way is that the Gherkin."

"You couldn't see that far."

"It's possible. Taking the bend in the river into account.".

"We're looking north."

"East."

"Never mind the river. That's Waterloo. And the Tower beyond."

"Bollocks."

"More like north-east."

"Well, that's certainly the London Eye."

Moira joined them. She laid a proprietary arm around Rachel's shoulders and claimed the attention of the group. "Hey, you lot, meet Walter the Warthog's creator."

Rachel cringed.

"Rachel Hines used to live here. Ray, these layabouts are my new students."

She recited their names: Santhya, Ahmed, Will, Rosie – but Rachel did not attempt to memorise the names or attach the names to the faces. She would remember Santhya, though; an Australian of Indian heritage, who had immediately launched into a description of her MA thesis for Rachel's benefit. As far as she could understand, the thesis was to do with animal imagery in aboriginal art and its influence on story-telling for children. This threw up a lot of questions which she wanted to voice but the noise in the room was mounting and Santhya's enthusiastic exposition didn't provide opportunities to intervene. Rachel was looking around for an escape when Santhya said something that caught her attention. "Your warthog is an example."

"Is he? An example? What of?"

"Yes. Walter is ogly."

"Ogly?"

"Yes. But you have made him beautiful inside. This is the secret of your success.!

Is it? wondered Rachel. She thought successful sales had much more to do with the large sums of money Malcolm had persuaded the publicity department to spend on promotion over many years. But she was flattered by Santhya's view. And she was right: that had been her idea from the start, to create an ugly hero. She drew him with a horribly toothy grin beneath unwieldy tusks and rampant bristles. Few of the characters he came across in his travels could see the appealing character hidden within his frightening exterior. Walter was loved, by those who could truly see him, for his good intentions, startling blunders and heart-warming outcomes.

Leaning towards Santhya so she could be heard, she said "Actually, I'm now dreaming up a character who is utterly beautiful."

"And good inside too?"

"Yes."

Next morning Rachel remembered, with some surprise, that she had described her ideas for Elfrida at length to the young woman who had paid her such flattering attention. She didn't want to be known any longer simply as the creator of Walter. She wanted to create something exclusive, not mass market. A limited edition, she elaborated. Perhaps woodcuts. Ten copies. Not more. Heavy parchment paper? Or light and flimsy? Lying in a box, a beautiful box lined with velvet. Could be made from cigar boxes, if she could find enough. A brass clasp. Like a casket? A set of woodcuts. Sealed in a box. This would be a visual pun on Elfrida's hermit life, spent in a cell.

"She devoted her life to prayer," she told her listener. "She prayed for the sins of the world from the age of 14."

"In my religion, too, we have such people."

The nice young woman's name was Santhya. Rachel felt pleased to have remembered it. Not that she was likely ever to meet her again.

"You seemed to have a good time last night," said Sally over their breakfast coffee.

"I did. What about you? I lost sight of you quite early on."

"Yes, wasn't it packed."

"I thought I was going to panic, in such a mass of people."

"You make it sound as though you've been a recluse in Devon for years and years."

"It feels like it. Not in bad way, though."

"Don't regret the move?"

"No, not at all." Was that strictly true? The party had been far more stimulating than anything she'd come across in Devon. Save for the forge... Could Robert make the clasps for the boxes? She pulled herself up abruptly. "I think I'll have a look at the V&A today, their medieval stuff."

The following day she went to the British Museum. "Cor, it's wonderful, this business of living in London!"

"Come back for good."

"I don't think I could afford to."

"Stay on longer, then."

There was another party on New Year's Eve to be given by new friends Sally had made. Jason and Jacinda lived in a converted warehouse somewhere off the Commercial Road. "You'll love them. They keep hens."

"Heavens above!"

"In their courtyard."

"Gracious!"

"In a henhouse modelled on a gypsy caravan."

"Can't wait."

"They also have two greyhounds."

"I'll take my sketch pad."

"Not to a party on their scale."

On arrival, Rachel understood why there'd be no chance of whipping out a sketch pad. It was hard enough to hold a glass steady. But she managed to take a photo of the greyhounds. gracefully posed side by side on adjacent floor cushions, their sleek heads turned towards the crowd, a mirror image of each other.

She was about to take another shot from a different angle when she heard a familiar voice. What she'd dreaded had happened. Malcolm was not with his wife in the country. He was at Jason and Jacinda's party. He had a girl at his side. The girl could have been Rachel herself, twenty years or so previously.

Rachel turned away swiftly, pocketing her phone.

ANGELA 13

The drip has started again. It must be raining outside. Still winter, I daresay. Nicolas did bring me another blanket but that seems ages ago, so it could be nearly spring. Good to believe so, in any case.

I shall try and think of something warming. Like hot chocolate. No! That's no good, I know. Thoughts of food and drink are to be avoided.

Find something safer.

Memories of summer days?

Yes. I'm at the landing window. The Leylandii hedge hides the cottage but I can see the Johnsons' garden. Lionel is in his straw hat, watering the neatly mown lawn. Ruth has her secateurs. She's got her lovely, open-ended, flower-gathering basket over one arm. I think it has a special name but I can't think of it at the moment. I always longed to have one, and to have a garden with two herbaceous borders. I'd wander down neatly edged grass paths between the borders, cutting long-stemmed flowers and laying them in my basket. There'd be butterflies and bees flitting around and about, and a heady scent of honeysuckle from the climbers – yes, clematis, too, and espalier pears - on the red brick wall. A walled garden. Well-tended by the gardeners. I was a Victorian lady of leisure.

In reality, I was the wife of Nicolas whose idea of gardening was to let everything grow. He probably still does. No reason why he should change, in this or in anything else. He was overjoyed when the idea of wilding came in.

I could have been a keen gardener, but he didn't trust me not to trim everything to within an inch of its life; his own words.

Back to the landing window, on a summer morning. The scene has changed. There's no sign of Lionel, nor of Ruth. The reason why I was drawn to the window is, at the very moment, mowing the lawn. Robert. Without a shirt. Brown muscled arms on the Hayter motor mower.

Robert is some kind of relation, recently appeared on the scene. The Johnsons are growing more fragile. He helps them out. I'm always hoping that he will knock on our door and need something. This only happened once.

"I don't like to disturb them. They're having their rest. Could you give me a glass of water?"

I gave him a glass of water with chunks of ice and a slice of lemon in it. I didn't give him the jug I'd made up, because I hoped he'd come back with the glass for a refill.

Now, in my underground cell, I try to recall his features and the sound of his voice. No good. All I can summon up is my response to his presence. Sheer, hopeless infatuation. What was it about Robert that I found so devastating? Animal magnetism? Whatever he had, Nicolas reacted badly to it.

He came up behind me as I stood at the door, chatting with Robert. We must have been there sometime before Nicolas got wind of it. I learnt a lot quickly. He'd recently returned from the States. His family had farmed in the area but had sold up. A newly-married, young couple had bought the house. Tom was in oil and away a lot. Lucy was lovely and made a great neighbour. Robert's parents had kept the milking parlour which Robert had converted into a forge. He'd given up banking in the City. Had he had some sort of breakdown perhaps? Anyrate, he wanted to indulge his passion for making things. On leaving school, he'd been apprenticed to a blacksmith. Now he was going to concentrate on decorative ironwork. And dogs. He loved dogs.

"I've always longed for a dog."

Robert didn't understand why I'd never had one. I couldn't begin to explain Nicolas to him. I didn't have to because there was Nicolas, pushing me away from the door and taking my place in the conversation.

"I hate dogs," said Nicolas. "You're the Johnsons' gardener?"

"Well, in a kind of way."

"Whatever you do, do not cut the Leylandii hedge."

"I don't plan to. I'm just helping Lionel and Ruth with the lawn."

I recognised the expression on Robert's face; a mixture of hurt, surprise and bafflement, which interaction with Nicolas usually produces in others. It was my habit to smooth the path between Nicolas and the outside world. On this occasion, I wanted Nicolas to be the extreme of his rude, didactic and controlling self. That way, Robert would understand my position and feel sorry for me.

I've always retained the smallest sliver of hope that Robert will guess that I'm not missing or dead, but that I continue to exist as Nicolas's captive wife. He'll come and rescue me. After all, I'm not far away.

Some hope! Better to think of hot chocolate.

RACHEL 13

The sight of Malcolm with his arm wrapped around the waist of her replacement had sent her back into one of the black moods she'd thought had gone for ever. Fortunately, on this occasion, she recovered fast. Conversations with people she didn't know at the two parties had given her a fresh perspective on her present life. She returned from London full of energy and enthusiasm for developing her Elfrida ideas. She had a plan. She would drop in on Lucy. She didn't need to do more sketches but she wanted to talk over the possibilities of creating what she called in her mind a 'precious artefact.' She imagined making just one to begin with: a treasure chest of a box, about six inches by eight, holding a sheaf of woodcuts set in intricate and richly coloured borders inspired by the illuminated manuscripts she'd seen in the British Museum and the Victoria and Albert. Lucy, although not a creator herself, was the centre of a hub of makers. She'd help Rachel find the people who would provide the things she might need –handmade paper, carpentry, blocks of wood, calligraphy, tapestry. After the depression the sight of Malcolm had induced, she was buoyed up by all the possibilities she'd explore.

Before contacting Lucy, she wanted to wander around the priory ruins, absorbing the atmosphere and thinking herself into the heart of the young girl who'd immured herself for a life of prayer. From the Johnsons' old Torridon papers, Rachel had learnt that Elfrida had not in fact been entirely solitary. Her cell was in two sections. The first chamber was the link to the outside world. Into this chamber came the anchorite's special servant to bring her sustenance and take away the detritus. A grille was set high in one wall and people would come to the grille to consult Elfrida. The Rev Ell, as Rachel called the builder of Torridon, likened this to a confessional. He quoted some of the success stories. Divers people suffering from ague of the mind left the blessed anchorite rejoicing and thanking the heavenly

Father for the cure. Rachel thought she'd become a kind of medieval counsellor.

A further door led into Elfrida's cell. It had originally been a hermit's cave, before the priory was built. The Rev Ell thought the cave was the reason the priory had been founded in the first place. There was a spring of holy water in the rock. No-one but Elfrida would ever enter this inner chamber. The young girl had entered and would never leave either inner or outer chamber ever again. The thought of this made Rachel shudder. To think that she might be able to find the actual place where Elfrida had spent thirty or more years ... - it would be a delicious horror to try.

She would wait for a day when she would have plenty of time. Nicolas was sometimes absent for a whole day, going to some auction or another. She would watch from the window at the top of the stairs, which looked over the car park hedge towards the barn where he kept his car. She could tell from what he was wearing whether he was just on a normal shopping trip or whether it was an auction day, in which case he took more care with his appearance. His camelhair coat with leather-clad buttons was a sure sign of a long day out

Towards the end of January, Rachel was passing the window on her way to the studio when she saw Nicolas going through the gate to his barn. He was wearing his auction-going coat. She felt suddenly empty. It was like standing on the highest level of the diving board, looking down at the water far below. She was ready but surely she would not jump.

She went downstairs and put on her boots and raincoat. She could at least walk down to the end of her garden before making a decision. After heavy rain, the clouds had rolled away to reveal blue sky. First, she'd make sure that Nicolas was not going to return to collect some forgotten item. Taking her time, she strolled down the garden to the spot where she and Oliver had gathered piles of hedge cuttings ready for the next bonfire. She stood there for a while, savouring the moment before she committed herself to trespass. There was no hurry. She gazed at the boundary between her garden and Nicolas's. Over the last months she'd mapped out a possible path into his territory. The first step was relatively easy: up and onto the boundary bank to stand in the cleared patch of the hedgerow thorn bushes, which they'd managed to create before being ordered to stop.

Once on the bank, she stood again for a while, taking in her isolation, thinking of Elfrida, her muse. What a decision it had been for the girl, to enter the priory, take possession of her cell, and carry through her vow. It had required huge determination – or blind faith and innocence? More likely it was desperation which drove her to her action. The life of an anchorite must have seemed like the best and only alternative to being married to her rapist. She'd had to seek permission from an abbot. That would have taken weeks. There was also a protracted ceremony to start with. She might have found lots of opportunities to turn back, to be persuaded by a parent or a churchman that this was not a good choice for a young girl. She had not turned back.

Unlike Elfrida, Rachel considered turning back. She imagined Nicolas appearing out of nowhere to find her in his garden, skirting his workshop, making for the ruins. What excuse could she possibly provide? Nothing feasible occurred to her.

She decided she did not need to locate Elfrida's cell. She could create her 'precious artefact' perfectly well without recourse to inspiration on the spot. Besides, nothing could possibly remain of a thirteenth century hermit's dwelling. She was on a fool's errand.

But even as she thought of retreat, she went forward, scrabbling down the bank, pushing her way through thorn bushes, beds of dried nettle stems, brambles and long grass until she was outside the workshop. Here was the chance to peer in through a dusty window to try and make out what occupied Nicolas for hours every day. Restoration of antiques, said Betty Middleton. Well, she could see him collecting antiques – she knew he did, his barn was full of what's known as 'brown' furniture and tea chests. But she could not see him mending anything. That would take patience.

She knew he did carry things between Torridon and the workshop. She'd watched him from her studio window, going up and down the section of garden that was visible, with objects piled up in the trailer of his ride-on mower – which, incidentally, was never used for mowing grass. She'd strained to make out what he was carrying through the binoculars she kept on her desk for the purpose. Full, black polythene sacks, mostly. The sacks must hold antiques, on their way from salerooms and back to salerooms, gaining dust and a little profit as they did so. That she could imagine.

With her hands held either side of her face, she created a dark shape on the glass of the workshop window through which she could see a wooden counter, not unlike the one in Rob's forge. Its surface was covered with the sort of things you find in a charity shop: candlesticks, jugs, clothes, pictures, books, it was hard to tell exactly what. Satisfied, she continued around the building on a path well-worn through the rampant undergrowth. A small outbuilding was tacked on the back, obviously a lavatory. It had a stove pipe on its roof, from which came a pungent smell of excrement. She hurried on.

She found herself in a maze of tumbledown walls and broken pillars - a cloister perhaps. The ground was uneven, she had to watch her step. Clumps of willow grew in dells. A distance ahead, she recognised the wall which she'd seen from the bridle track on the other, public side. She had been struck by the way Nicolas had rebuilt it to a good height with cement blocks. Another instance of his passion for privacy. She brought to mind one of the maps the Rev Ell had drawn, which showed the cell and the public path. But however much ground she covered in her search she could not find any hint of a ruined cell.

Disappointed, she retraced her steps towards the workshop. The ground became hillocky. From the top of one mound she could see the stove pipe on the outbuilding she'd seen at the back of the workshop. It was about twenty yards away. Below her lay a grassy dell. A muddy path skirted the far slope. She guessed it would lead to the workshop. She'd begun to slither down the wet grass of the slope to reach the path when she heard the sound of someone approaching. She felt her heart thudding in her chest. She dug in her heels and stood as upright as the slippery slope allowed. It was Nicolas who appeared on the path. They stared at each other, transfixed.

Time passed. Rachel tried to summon reasons for her presence but said nothing. She watched Nicolas emerge from his trance. He bent down and picked up a stone. She watched his arm draw back. She turned to scrabble back up the slope but she could not get a foothold. She fell forward. It was as though the earth had come up and hit her on the back of her head. She tried to make sense of this. At the same time, she knew Nicolas had gripped her left leg by the ankle and was pulling her down the slope. She tried to grab at the marshy grass but failed because she was struck again. Then she knew nothing.

ANGELA 14

Extraordinary occurrence today. Commotion outside. Nicolas was banging about as he does when he loses his temper. This went on for some time. I couldn't make out from the muffled sounds what on earth he could be doing. Then he unlocked the door and dragged something into the room. It looked like a rolled-up carpet and I was excited. A lovely surprise. Was it my birthday? Or might it be Christmas?

He said, "Look after this." He put his foot to the side of the bundle and pushed it out of the way of the door so he could go out. It looked as if it was too heavy to move more than an inch or two. He returned at once with a basin of water and a bag of cotton wool balls. "Clean it up." He put his hand on the back of his head.

I could tell he was in the kind of state he gets into when things go wrong. It's as though he's all but lost the power of speech. He's in a panic and tries to do too many things at the same time.

"All right," I said soothingly. "What is it?"

He'd already gone out and locked the door. I could hear him sliding the bolts into place.

I sat and looked at the bundle, savouring the moment of the unknown, so rare in my monotonous, predictable life! I could see that whatever it was wasn't a carpet. It was something wrapped in one of our Indian bedspreads. Then, bless me, the bundle moaned.

I know I took the name of our Lord in vain. I usually manage to change Christ to Crikey but on this occasion I didn't.

I went over and peeled back a corner of the bedspread. The bundle was a woman with huge staring eyes, a bloody mass of hair, and a scream coming out of her, such a scream as I've never heard before. She was looking at me and screaming in utter fear and horror.

This was how Rachel and I first met.

PART TWO

DAY ONE

Robert found it hard to refuse to take on a dog, which is why he had such a motley collection of hounds to take for walks. He'd be in the forge's yard at 8 in the morning, ready to receive the dogs as they were dropped off by their owners for the whole day. Usually, Rufus the dachshund was first to arrive, followed by Bertie the arthritic bulldog. Lucy the Irish wolfhound was a regular and just as regularly late. She and Rufus were great friends. Robert enjoyed watching them together; they clearly thought they lived in much the same stratosphere, with Rufus lodged a meter or two higher. With hooded eyes and long nose, he had a way of looking down on everything. He managed to give this impression even when the object he was regarding was well above his head, as Lucy was.

Sometimes there was also Sam the springer spaniel. He belonged to Tina who had inherited him aged 18 months. Sam had never had the benefit of a firm upbringing, so Bob forgave his wild excitability. The walks were always much less stressful when Tina didn't have to leave Sam with him. There were one or two other dogs he accepted on the occasions when he was particularly worried about money, but they were much more like paid chores than animals. For a dog called Chin Pin he had a particular antipathy, though perhaps it was the bitch's owner that irritated him more than the temperamental animal itself.

He knew people liked to see him and his pack of hounds walking around the lanes. They'd smile and wave, giving him the thumbs-up. This had been all part of his recovery after his London years and there was no reason to give up. On the contrary, he had a very good reason to go on. Selling honey from his bees was seasonal; the forge was little more than a hobby; the money from the sale of his parents' farmhouse to Tom and Lucy had taken a severe knock in the financial crash, as had the proceeds from his City life. Dog-walking brought in a little extra. Better still, he enjoyed the dogs' company. He forgot his money worries when he took the pack out walking. This didn't mean all worry was banished from his mind. His main concern remained: Rachel.

At the exact moment when Rachel slithered down the bank into the priory grounds, Bob was at the beginning of the bridle track near the Middletons' farmhouse, not quite a mile away. He'd decided that morning to take the pack on the long circuit from the forge, onto the village road, then down the valley to the T-junction where the entrance to Priory Cottage and Torridon lay. He'd continue to Priory Farm and then back via the bridle track and the valley lane. Various reasons for his choice of direction had formed overnight at the back of his mind. He told himself that he needed to look carefully at Torridon's sign so he could take its size and style in mind when he came to make the one for Priory Cottage. He wanted the cottage sign to fit in with its setting and yet stand out with a kind of restrained elegance. Lurking underneath this reason was the hope that he might just come across the owner of the cottage.

Thoughts of Rachel had filled his mind since the early autumn when he'd first seen and fallen for her. He used to think that this business of falling in love was always mutual. It had to be. A simultaneous transformation, the birth of a new relationship. He'd had lots of girlfriends. He'd talked about loving each of them, deeply, as long as they lasted. He realised he hadn't really loved them, not in the way he found he loved Rachel. He'd had no idea of how it hurt to really love someone, and not have that feeling returned. It puzzled and irked him that she was so cool towards him. He was not used to receiving such a chilly response. He even wondered if he'd made a severe blunder that he'd been unaware of. He kept replaying the few times they'd been together. Nothing in the encounters seemed to him to present a reason for her coolness. This morning, as he followed the dogs on their enthusiastic investigation of every smell they came across, he went over yet again the moment of first meeting Rachel. He'd got up from the sofa in Tina's pottery studio to greet her as she approached. If he had done nothing wrong, then was it simply that she'd taken an immediate dislike to him, in the same way as he disliked Chin Pin's owner? This had never happened to him in his life before. Or, if it had, he'd been blithely unaware of it. He was the sort of person everyone liked. Up to now. Up to Rachel.

"Sam! Lucy! Chin Pin! Bert!" The dogs were clambering up the bank on the priory side of the bridle track, following a run made by a fox, rabbits or a badger. He got them down with difficulty, disentangling their leads as he did so.

He had to meet her, just one-to-one, and find out what he'd done or not done. It was imperative to discover. She was the one person he'd ever met with whom he'd felt at home at once. It was a feeling of recognition. She was what he'd been longing for. It was like reaching the finishing tape in a marathon. Not a way station but a terminus. Such strength of feeling – and nothing in return.

He had now passed the high wall that Nicolas Clarkson had built up at the end of the priory ruins. Usually, he let the dogs run free once he'd gone past Clarkson's boundary. Today, he kept them all on their leads. They were feverishly excited by a scent they'd picked up. Perhaps a fox had passed by. Rufus and Chin Pin were scrabbling in the ditch, snuffling the ground. Sam was half way up the bank, barking excitedly. Lucy was pawing at the hedge, loosening stones which fell on Bert who sat panting at Bob's feet with his tongue lolling out, a trail of slobber falling onto Bob's walking boots. Sam slipped his leash, bounded to the top of the bank, through the hedge and disappeared into the field that bordered the ruins. Bob whistled and swore and shouted. He must prevent Sam getting into Clarkson's land. In the past, the overenthusiastic spaniel had suffered vicious kicks. On the other hand, he could be following a trail made by Rachel. She might well have cut across this field to the track. Betty said she liked local walks. If Sam was, nose down, on his way to Rachel's garden, it would present a fantastic opportunity. He and the pack would follow. He was just beginning to imagine the possible encounter with Rachel when he heard a distant, angry shout from the direction of the priory. Sam made a kind of handbrake turn in a shower of stones. He raced back to Bob with his tail between his legs.

Bob had to smile at the sight. "Not quite so brave now, then?" he said, ruffling the spaniel's floppy ears.

With Sam back on his lead and all leads disentangled and fastened securely on the master loop, Bob and the pack continued on their way. He wouldn't let the dogs run free until they'd reached the woods.

Angela was desperate to make the woman stop screaming. It felt as though a power tool was drilling a hole from ear to ear through her skull. She was helpless in the face of such terror, especially as she understood that she herself was the cause. Why that should be, she couldn't fathom. If, as she assumed, the woman had been abducted by Nicolas, then the woman should be very glad to see another human being in the cell. She herself had managed all this time on her own with only Nicolas for company and that was for a very short time each day. Sometimes, he even missed a day. He rarely sat down on her single chair to talk with her. When he did, it was a monologue. He didn't expect an answer. He didn't *want* an answer. If she offered a thought of her own, it usually annoyed him intensely and he'd get up and leave. Best to be his silent listener. No wonder her voice came out in such a croak.

She cleared her throat several times before speaking. "Don't be alarmed."

The woman's scream grew even more piercing in pitch.

"There's nothing to be afraid of."

Her words were inaudible. The cell was filled with the scream.

Angela decided the best thing to do was to demonstrate

she was harmless. She took a couple of cotton wool balls from the pack Nicolas had brought, dipped them in the basin of water and squeezed them out. Then she bent over the woman on the floor, who was doing her utmost to roll closer to the wall. The scream, through lack of breath, had turned into short, panting shrieks.

"It's alright. I want to help you. It looks as though you've bashed your head."

Angela reached down to dab at the woman's hair but she reacted like an animal being attacked. She scrunched herself up in the foetal position, her hands clasping her head, her forearms tight against her ears.

"Oh well," said Angela. "Suit yourself. But I can tell you, it's best to clean a wound. It's easy for things to go bad in here."

She returned to her chair where she'd been sitting before the intrusion. This would take time to sort out. It was such an extraordinary happening that she scarcely believed it was real. Sometimes she did fall into a waking dream. This could be an instance of that phenomenon. A woman joining her in the cell. A dream. Or might it be a nightmare.

The woman was definitely real, though. She was muttering something. Angela leant close. It sounded like a prayer. *In the name of Jesus Christ, in the name of Jesus Christ,* repeated in a rapid stutter She was surprised to recall that this is what you say to be saved from an evil spirit.

"There's no Jesus Christ in here, I can tell you. I'd have been saved yonks ago. It's just me. I'm Angela, Nicolas's wife." She was pleased to hear her voice sounding almost normal with all the practice it was having. "You're not by any chance a second Mrs Clarkson?" She wouldn't put it past Nicolas to have a living copy of herself inhabiting Torridon. It was something that she'd expected to happen for a long time. She'd be glad if he did find someone for the role, from all points of view save one. Her replacement would provide all the functions she had fulfilled while above ground. The single penalty would be he'd no longer want to keep her alive, below ground.

If this person who'd joined her in her cell was a second Mrs Clarkson, what would that mean for the chances for *both* of them staying alive? She turned this thought over in her mind while she regarded her companion. She found it hard to concentrate in this utterly new situation, although the incomer had stopped panicking. She was slumped against the wall by the door, blood drying in the matted hair on the crown of her head. A purplish-streak in the blonde locks that lay about her face was not blood, as she'd first thought, but dye. That, and her baggy, colourful, ethnic trousers, made her look unusual. How on earth had Nicolas come across her? And what had she done, to cause him to punish her? She wouldn't have come at him with a knife. Could she be a Fine Arts student? No, not a student. Most unlikely. She looked about forty; at a guess, some ten to fifteen years younger than she was herself. Perhaps an art school teacher? Angela had a host of questions lined up to ask, but she'd wait for the poor woman to recover from her shock.

Although her head was pounding and she felt dizzy and sick, Rachel found she could uncurl. She struggled into a sitting position, her back against the wall. She took in that she had not been cast back to the Middle Ages to join Elfrida in her cell. The ghastly apparition was not a ghost but the wreck of a woman wearing 21st century clothing, shapeless jogging bottoms and a grey sweatshirt. The two of them were in a cave-like room. It contained a camp bed, a chair, a table, a lidded bucket. There was no window but there was an electric bulb dangling from a flex tacked to the centre of the low, cement ceiling which matched the cement block walls. The wall she leant against held a big, wooden door. High in the corner of this wall was a round hole, the size of a vacuum cleaner's hose. The room seemed to have been built around a recess in a damp cave. The skeletal woman looked like a wilder version of one of those unfortunates who sleep rough in city doorways.

She was asking her questions, one after the other. "How did you get hurt? Was it Nicolas? He's not a violent man. Did you fall? Do tell me what happened? Where were you? Were you visiting his workshop?"

The skeletal woman sounded desperate for answers. She gabbled on. "Are we below his workshop? I've always thought so. He dug a pit somewhere around here, for a heat pump. Or so he said. But when he put me here, I went over things. I went back in my mind and I reckon that before the knife event he'd been planning this for some time."

"You're the wife?" Of course, thought Rachel, it was beginning to make sense. Nicolas must have kept her here for years. She found it disturbing to think that she'd been living happily at Priory Cottage all this time, while Mrs Clarkson had been incarcerated at the bottom of the garden next door. "You're *Angela*? The wife who went missing?"

"Yes, I told you that a moment ago but never mind, you've been concussed so it's no surprise you're a bit groggy. Let me bathe the cut. Did you fall or were you pushed?" She smiled, revealing a gap in her row of yellow front teeth. She had difficulty with her s's and Rachel had trouble understanding her.

"Sorry?"

"What's your name?"

"Rachel. Lots of people I've met thought you were dead."

"Good as!"

Rachel was amazed by how happy she sounded. Imprisoned here for years! She herself felt ghastly, physically sick and mortally afraid. The reality of the situation, as it became clearer, filled her with dread.

"But you must have been down here for years!"

She recalled Betty Middleton filling her in on local background. She'd described Nicholas as being 'unfortunate' as he'd 'lost' his wife a few years ago. Betty wouldn't elaborate on what she meant by 'lost'. Other people had told her that his wife had gone off with another man – *no surprise there*, they added with a knowing glint in their eyes. Someone else had been convinced Nicolas had killed Angela and buried her in the ruins. But Rachel had dismissed that idea as implausible. The version she'd trusted was shared by both Lucy and Robert: Angela Clarkson had been registered as a Missing Person, and still was missing.

Now she wasn't, at least as far as Rachel was concerned. She was in the cell that had once been Elfrida's, now excavated and restored and accessed somehow – she wasn't sure how - from Nicolas's workshop.

Moira stopped Sally at the main entrance to the flats and asked if she'd heard yet from Rachel.

Sally regretted telling Moira that she hadn't had either an email, a phone call, a text or – the occasional surprise – a postcard thanking Sally for the Christmas visit. She hadn't expected a quick response, as she'd taken into account Rachel's shock at seeing Malcolm on New Year's Eve, especially as he was with a younger, blonder version of Ray herself. Sally understood what effect this had on her friend. However stalwart Ray was in the face of life's vicissitudes – their shared phrase for such setbacks – on this latest occasion she had seemed extremely upset. This would explain the deviation from her usual behaviour.

"No, not yet," she replied. She might be understanding about the silence, but she was also becoming resentful. It was up to Rachel to ring her; not for her to make the running. There were certain unstated rules in their long friendship, one of which was that neither should be made to seem needy.

"I hope nothing's wrong." Moira looked concerned. "Rachel usually puts a card – one of her own – in our mail box very soon after our Boxing Day party."

"Mostly, yes, she is good at thank-you's." Sally put it down to her upbringing. She'd met Rachel's parents in the past. They were academics who seemed to be happier in their own subjects – father in medieval history, mother in 19th century economic history – than in parenting. Rachel and her brother Oliver had grown up in an absent-minded fog with infrequently applied standards of politeness. "But she can be haphazard. She doesn't always keep up with people or ideas."

"Except Walter," put in Moira. "She's stuck at that for years."

"Not any longer," said Sally. "She's onto something else now."

"Oh yes, you're right. Some legend or other? Santhya was telling me. Perhaps it unsettled her, being back in London. Seeing us getting on so well with our lives."

"Oh, I don't think that's the sort of thing that would worry her," said Sally. Typical Moira to make a point about her own success.

They went their separate ways, Sally to see an Oscar-winning film and Moira to the lift.

Walking towards the bus stop, Sally admitted to herself that she agreed with Moira. She, too, had come to the conclusion that Rachel regretted her decision to give up everything and move to that godforsaken spot in the country where she knew no-one. The only person she seemed to spend any time with was the wife of the (gorgeous) blacksmith. She had Robert's number. In a day or two she would ring him on the pretext of enquiring about the progress of the Priory Cottage sign. She could casually ask if he or Lucy had heard from Rachel; it was now towards the end of January and high time to check Rachel had not sunk into a depression again, a repeat of the one that had provoked her move in the first place.

Oliver suggested to Matt that, now he was home again, they might invite Rachel for a meal in Exeter. "I owe her," he said, flipping through the pages of their favourite cookery book.

"I thought it was the other way around. You were always up there working away with a chain saw in her garden. You told me that you'd be in credit with her for ages."

"Yes, but." Oliver used their shorthand for reluctant agreement. "I felt bad that she was on her own for Christmas."

"Didn't she go to Sally in London?"

"Yes, but. Not family."

"Who's got family?"

Silence. Both of them realised they'd strayed onto a topic best avoided. Matt had family who he'd recently left yet again.

"What about," Oliver began, turning the pages fast, "what about …" He wanted to find something to cook that would bring Matt around to the prospect of an evening with Rachel. "What about that one we did for the gang in the summer?"

"The paella?"

"Was it paella? Sure it wasn't a cassoulet?"

"Paella. And if it wasn't, let's do it anyway - for poor Rachel."

Oliver heard the bite of sarcasm in Matt's tone. Poor Rachel indeed! He didn't want his sister to be considered a subject for pity. She wasn't! She was fantastic. Hugely successful, attractive, fun. A wonderful sister. Matt was jealous, that was the thing; jealous if Oliver ever spent time with her. Which was a bit rich, seeing that Matt could go home to his wife and children without pay-back.

"Paella it is," said Oliver. With a little nostalgia for his single life, he read aloud the long list of ingredients. How complicated it could be to share domesticity. "When will it be? Let's look at our diaries."

Besides their mutual diary, Oliver had two others: one kept by the receptionist at the consulting rooms and one kept at home for personal appointments. Matt's life as an osteopath was organised, or rather disorganised, on scraps of paper. His phone was in constant use. Their mutual diary was an elaborate affair: each year, whether they were able to be together or not, they bought a lavishly illustrated production from a London museum or gallery. Choosing one each year took days. Choosing a date for Rachel's meal would also take a very long time.

Nicolas poured himself a whisky. His hands were trembling. He was exhausted. Beside him on the kitchen floor was the mattress he'd pulled off the spare bed. It was brand new and hard to handle. He'd bought it years ago when the police had kept calling in that annoying way, with question after question. Each time they called, he'd fielded the questions adeptly - he was proud of himself - but back they came, bloodhounds after a scent. The issue then had been about their bedroom arrangements. He'd taken his old camp bed from the loft down to Angela's new abode, as well as the mattress from the spare room's bed. Why, asked the police, doesn't this bed have a mattress? Well, answered Nicolas thinking fast, we had a niece staying, a little niece, not very old, two? who wet the bed. Oh yes, said the police, and when was that? I'm afraid I can't remember. I'm afraid my wife keeps track of things like that. That had been true.

He poured more whisky.

That first time, he'd replaced the mattress he'd given Angela with a brand-new one. The important thing had been to keep everything going as normal, given the circumstances of a missing wife. It had gone on for two years at least before the case was shelved. Had it not been for budget cuts, the case might still be going.

He took another gulp, feeling it warming his gullet.

Now here he was again, having to think up not just his next steps but how he should respond to the questioning that would surely follow. He'd hoped to god it wouldn't be the same bloody detective, Sam Frightful, Nicolas had called him. His real name was Fulford. Detective Sergeant Sam Fulford. Thick as two short planks. Or maybe not.

How long would it take for people to get wind of Rachel's absence? Betty bloody Middleton would come around asking. He knew she often took Rachel to Saturday market. He had five days before that might happen.

For fuck's sake, why did the bloody woman have to go snooping about the Priory? She'd got what she deserved, that was for certain. He should have thrown the stone harder, but he was barely thinking at the time. It had been a quick, natural reaction to a trespasser, not a premeditated act. In any case, she wouldn't die. He was not a killer.

And that was going to be the problem. He had two women on his hands now. He'd have his work cut out.

He'd have just one more snifter before getting the fucking mattress to the cell. Rachel would have to sleep on something. She was going to get this bloody expensive, never used mattress. She'd need food! Water! His life was going to be an even greater drag, looking after two women. Either he'd become even more of a slave, or else he'd have to become a killer. Perhaps if they simply died? Poisoned? That would be death, not murder. He could bury them both.

But no! He would not lose Angela. She was his wife. Bloody Rachel, buying Priory Cottage, sticking her nose in. Worse still, he found her alluring. an uncomfortable and unaccustomed feeling.

He thought nostalgically of the period between the Johnsons' demise and today. He'd had a clear run. Torridon was his domain, with nobody next door. He was in luck. If only the heirs had continued to quarrel, obstructing the settlement and sale of the place, he could have gone on living happily, undisturbed. Even if Priory Cottage had gone without dispute to Robert, all would have been fairly well. But then there was that history with Robert. He'd done that thing with the Johnsons' money, he remembered – being a City whizz kid, showing off, losing it all in the crash - and they'd cut him out of their wills. Then Robert had moved back to Devon and become so helpful to them. Tbe bloody man was back in the Johnsons' good books. They told Nicolas that Robert would definitely be his next door neighbour one day. But they'd forgotten to reinstate Robert, which led to all those wrangles and delays over the house sale. Which suited him well enough until onto the scene came bloody Rachel Hines. Nothing ever worked out right. Robert was not a bad chap and, if the useless Johnsons had remembered to put him back in their wills, he'd have been left the cottage. He would have taken hints to stay clear. He had never asked to see his workshop, why would he suddenly want to?

Whatever happens in life, sure as hell, it always throws up trouble - trouble caused by other people. As a child, he was determined to live on a desert island when he grew up. Two women holed up at the bottom of the garden! Robinson Crusoe never had to contend with that.

He dragged the mattress out of the kitchen and left it at the side of the house while he fetched the sit-on mower and trailer from the stables. It was almost dark and he could barely see the drive which led around the side of the house, through his wonderfully overgrown garden to the workshop, then around the building to the back. From here, it was a matter of manhandling the mattress out of the trailer and dragging it into the dell in the ruins which contained on its far side the oak door to Angela's abode, set into the slope and well hidden by ivy and wild clematis. He'd come this way at least once a day for several years and the path was well-trodden through the undergrowth but it was narrow and muddy, and brambles kept snagging the mattress. Swearing brought him no relief. Red-hot anger swirled in his brain. Bloody women.

While Angela gabbled on, clearly thrilled with the chance to talk, Rachel had become aware of a number of urgent bodily needs. She badly wanted to pee. To have a cup of tea. To take an aspirin. To wash and change her clothes. To lie down on her own bed in her own cottage. Only the first of these would be possible; Angela surely must have the means to relieve herself. That's what the bucket in the corner could be for. She would need to ask any moment. It couldn't be put off much longer. But to ask an absolute stranger if she could pee in a bucket in the corner of her room, even if it was a kind of dungeon... could she do such a thing? She would have to, unless Nicolas appeared to take her to a proper loo within the next few minutes.

She regarded her situation as temporary. She'd had a kind of accident and found herself in Elfrida's cell. Yes, Nicolas had held a stone and she had fallen, but she'd slipped on wet grass. Her next door neighbour would never have flung a stone at her. He was odd, but he certainly wasn't belligerent. He'd always been extremely polite to her. Maybe not to others; she'd been told lots of stories. She'd known she'd be in trouble if he caught her wandering about the priory ruins, but not to the extent of being held captive. That was beyond imagination.

He must have carried her into Elfrida's cell to lie there until she recovered consciousness. Now she'd come to, he'd let her go.

"Angela. Sorry to interrupt but do you think Nicolas will be back in a minute?"

"Why would he come back today?"

"For me!"

"For you?"

"Yes."

"Why on earth? He'd brought me food and water only minutes before your arrival. We won't see him again until tomorrow."

"*Tomorrow?*"

Angela proceeded to tell Rachel the usual routine. "First, I know that it's another day when the light goes on. Nicolas is very clever with electrics. There's an automatic timer in the workshop. Without the electric light it would always be dark in here. I can breathe because air comes in through that funnel." She pointed to a small, round hole high up in the wall behind her. Immediately Rachel felt hot and breathless. She thought of the limited supply of oxygen the two of them were sharing. Angela continued, "He comes in at some point during the light hours to do the chores. He brings food and water once or twice a day. He takes away the clothes that need washing but I have to keep that to the barest minimum. His main job is to empty the bucket."

"The bucket! Yes, I wondered – "

"Do you need it? Don't mind me."

"I'd rather wait."

"You'll have to wait a long time. As I said, he won't be back until tomorrow."

"I can't wait. I must get home."

"Home! How lovely to have a home. Are you happy in the cottage? The Johnsons loved it."

Rachel didn't answer. She was beginning to understand her situation.

Angela continued, "You musn't think you'll ever get out of here. We're in it for life, and we should be glad about that."

Rachel looked at her in consternation.

"You don't want to be killed, do you?"

Rachel's mind whirled.

"What do you think Nicolas can do about you, except keep you here?"

Rachel was unable to speak.

"Do you think he'll let you back to lovely Priory Cottage to tell your friends all about your kind neighbour Mr Clarkson, shoving you into a dungeon with – remember her? – his missing wife, Mrs Angela Clarkson?"

Rachel felt her heart pounding within her rib cage. At the same time, she knew she must get to the bucket at once. With one hand on the wall for balance, she struggled to her feet, pulling down her trousers and pants with her other hand as she did so. A few stumbling steps took her towards the bucket.

Angela got there first and took the lid off. She held Rachel steady and helped her sit down. Poor Rachel, she thought. It does take some getting used to. Normally she paid no attention to the smell. Now she was aware of it, as though a visitor to Torridon's lavatory had discovered she hadn't pulled the plug. How weird to become suddenly house-proud! And how glad she'd be to take care of Rachel. She'd need all the care and attention that Angela had never had the chance to give anyone else ever before. Except, of course, Nicolas.

Nicolas let the mattress fall to the ground outside the entrance door. He used the hazel branch he kept hidden beneath a holly bush, for holding back the curtain of ivy and clematis while he fitted the biggest key from his full key ring into the lock. The massive door opened with its usual creak, and would crash shut if not held. He looked around for the stone he used as a prop but it was not to be found. He'd thrown it at Rachel, he remembered, as well as a lot of smaller stones. He had to hunt for a replacement. His temper was rising dangerously again; he recognised the hot, warning pressure building behind his eyes. Luckily it didn't take long to find a decent stone which held the door open wide enough to carry the mattress over the deep sill. In he went, for the *third* time today! He dumped the mattress on the floor so that he could close and lock the door, before slamming the iron bar in place and padlocking it for extra security. He sat down to catch his breath on the chair he kept in this first chamber, just for this purpose. The question now was: should he keep Rachel in the inner cell with Angela if there was room on her floor for the mattress? Or should they be separated? Women when they get together are the very limit. He could keep Rachel in this outer cell, where she'd have the benefit of the narrow grille that let in air and light. That would be giving her a luxury mostly denied to Angela. He only let Angela into this larger, lighter cell on special occasions. Angela did like her treats. No, he couldn't give his next door neighbour better treatment than his wife. That wouldn't do at all. Rachel would share Angela's cell. That would be fit punishment for snooping. After all, he had been punishing Angela for the last three years. *Attempted manslaughter* were the words he used to keep her docile.

What a business it had been the first time. Nicolas hoped that the experience gained with Angela's disappearance would help him this time. However, this time was totally different. It was unpremeditated. Unplanned! The bloody Priory Cottage woman had forced his hand.

So had Angela, come to think of it. What a shock it had been, all that time ago, to see her coming at him with the biggest knife from the knife set on the counter. He was convinced she really did intend to do him harm. He was sure she would have done. Her expression was murderous. She was yelling at him in a rage he'd never witnessed before. She would have slit his throat if he hadn't grabbed her, forced her to the ground, grabbed the knife, bound her up with her own tights. Parcel tape across her mouth. Later, in the workshop, a roll of silver tape did a better job.

He recalled his fright and indecision. He'd been taken by surprise. He'd no idea she had built up such resentment against him, with no obvious cause. She was unbalanced. He managed to keep her bound and gagged in the workshop while he thought out his strategy. Perhaps he didn't remember clearly but it seemed from this distance so easy. Angela had no circle of friends. Only Betty Middleton had enquired and that hadn't been for at least a week. He'd had plenty of time to make the hermit's cell foolproof. There'd been two interconnecting chambers from the start, the inner one more like a cave. He fitted a couple of heavy oak doors he'd bought years before from a reclamation yard. Keys, bolts and chains were not a problem;

he had a stock of such ironmongery. He drilled a hole through the wall between the two chambers and fitted a pipe to let air from the existing grille into the inner chamber. He composed and practised his story, Betty Middleton being his first test. She called for Angela to go with her to Saturday market. He'd put on a long mournful face. "I'm afraid she can't. She's left me."

That became the accepted story. He led anyone who asked after Angela's whereabouts to think she'd gone off with another man. No-one was surprised. After three weeks, he reported her missing to the police. By that time, their routine had been established. Angela was safely within the hermit's cell with a great deal of vegetation hiding the entrance and patches of giant nettles springing up along the semi-underground path between the back of the workshop and the cell.

As it turned out, Detective Sergeant Fulford was satisfied that Angela had gone off with a man called Dennis. Nicolas's creation was based on Angela's solicitor boss. They did search the house but by then Nicolas had prepared a likely trail for them to follow: suitcases taken, wardrobe depleted, empty bottles piled up, everything to demonstrate a runaway wife and an abandoned husband going to pieces.

He could enact this again, in a way appropriate to the new cast of characters. He'd say he'd seen Rachel getting into a car driven by a man he didn't recognise. A flight bag had been put in the boot.

Feeling better after his sit-down, he got up to unlock the door into the inner cell. He would have to be quick about the business of getting the mattress in without the women getting out. It seemed unlikely they'd have the strength. One of them was a pathetic wraith who'd never been up to much. The other had been unconscious; might still be so.

As he opened the door, he saw that his blasted neighbour was using the bucket. He thought of retreat. Best to go on forward, though, and act as though he hadn't noticed. But he couldn't help registering her long legs, first seen last summer emerging from tantalisingly tiny shorts. The sight elicited a reaction that Angela had always failed to do.

"Honestly! Nicolas! Can't you show a little respect?" Angela's voice was unusually loud and determined.

"Sorry," he said. "I thought this would do for her." It annoyed him to sound so meek. Like an obedient husband being host to a friend of his wife's.

"But there isn't room! She can't sleep in here. Leave the mattress out there."

Nicolas had already laid the mattress on the floor alongside Angela's bed. It filled all the available space left by the table, the chair and the bucket. That would do, and he'd make sure it did.

Rachel looked with utter dismay at the mattress. This was not going to be a temporary imprisonment. She could not believe it was happening.

DAY TWO

Rachel could hear the steady drip of water coming from somewhere above and behind her head. She couldn't understand why the bedroom ceiling had sprung a leak. With the help of many workmen, she'd made the cottage sound. The whole project had eaten into the money she'd made by selling her London house and buying in the country. On her return from staying with Sally over Christmas and New Year, she'd dared to look at her bank balance. Her sums had been overoptimistic. She would have to take the job that Charlie the landlord of the pub had offered her, as well as get on fast with her ideas for Elfrida. She'd have to adapt these, moving away from the elaborate Fine Art project she'd been visualising towards something closer to her usual style, aiming for another Walter and big sales. This would take much ingenuity. She might not manage it.

With these thoughts, and with eyes opening onto unrelieved blackness, it dawned on her that she was not in her Priory Cottage bedroom. Nor was she in Sally's Battersea flat. Tentatively she laid a hand on the side of her head near the crown. The sticky mass of hair confirmed the sequence of events she was now remembering. Nicolas Clarkson had hurled a stone at her and knocked her out. She'd come to in the very place that she'd been looking for: Elfrida's cell. It was inhabited by the first Mrs Clarkson. It seemed likely that Nicolas intended to make her the second inhabitant. They were both alive, prisoners in a damp, dark cave.

She sat up with difficulty. Every part of her ached. This was an appalling situation and she could not accept it. She would use all her skills to persuade Nicolas to let her go. Failing that, there must be a way to escape. She'd work on it.

Angela stirred. With a strange mixture of feelings, she

realised that she was not alone any longer. Rachel was beside her on the floor, waking up from a deep, night-long sleep. She herself had only just slipped into a short nap, having spent most of the night awake while Rachel lay warm under the blanket which she, Angela, had donated from the goodness of her heart. The newcomer would have to learn what life was like down here. Cold and damp. Nicolas would have to produce another blanket, better still a duvet, otherwise Queen Rachel would complain.

Forgive me, Lord, she added. Recently, she'd been engaging the deity she'd been brought up to believe in, in an almost continuous conversation. The only trouble was that he failed to answer. Maybe that was because, during her years as a married woman, she'd entirely lost her faith. Even if her life hadn't been filled with joy, it was at least bearable with the occasional highlight. She hadn't felt the need for anything "out there". In her imprisonment, she'd turned back to the Christian God she knew well in childhood. She needed to trust that there was something beyond her miserable human existence. *All things work together for good to them that love God.* St Paul's words written in her prayer book by her godmother were very comforting. She needed St Paul's reassurance just as much as the Romans did. She'd been Mary in a primary school nativity play and ever afterwards had strived to be as meek. *Be it unto me according to thy words.* She tried to become a better person: compassionate, charitable, forgiving. But she only had Nicolas to practise on. Now she had Rachel as well. Already she was failing. She was judging the newcomer too hastily, basing her view on the way she spoke.

It had been such a treat to talk with a companion. The poor woman had no idea what lay before her. She actually believed that Nicolas was going to let her out, first of all to the lavatory and after that back to her cottage and normal life. What a hope! Just imagine! She was in for a rude awakening.

Angela reminded herself that she'd suffered from similar

delusions at the beginning. She'd thought Nicolas would let her go any minute. He'd regret his actions. He wasn't a bad man. He was not the sort to keep anyone prisoner, and he would never have kept her locked up here were it not for her one and only, wild and incredible offence. It had taken him completely by surprise. She could bring his expression to mind, and she often did. Sheer disbelief and horror. To witness his abject horror had been satisfaction enough, without going further. But momentum carried her forward. Now she accepted her punishment because she deserved it. *Forgive me, Lord.*

She often replayed the nightmare sequence, which she was unable to interrupt or change. The knife set standing in the corner of the kitchen counter. Her hand on the biggest knife, steel-handled, never yet used. She maintained the conviction that she would never have gone further than hold the knife in her trembling hand. She would never be able to plunge a knife into a living body, let alone her husband's. But Nicolas must have thought otherwise. He grabbed her by the wrists. There was an almighty struggle but he was far stronger than she was. The knife grazed his shoulder. A mere scratch but there was a lot of blood and he would never trust her again. She was mad, he said. The police would charge her with attempted murder. An unprovoked attack. She was now paying the price for her stupid loss of control. So silly of her! To think she'd put up with Nicolas's ways for so many years, to let her rage consume her over a tiny incident; she could barely remember what it was that set her off. And she didn't need to remember because all that was long past. Water under the bridge. Now she just had to live her life quietly without upsetting him. She could do that, no trouble at all.

Just so long as the even tempo of her life in the cell wasn't upset by the newcomer. Maybe Rachel had been sent to her as a trial. Her patience was to be tested. If she passed the test, would there be a reward? On earth, or not until heaven? And would there be a heaven?

Angela resolved to play safe. She'd be good and kind. Rachel was her opportunity.

"Stan, pay attention a minute, will you. I want to tell you something not halfway strange."

"Get on with it, then."

"Well, you know I was up early with the calves?"

"Ay."

"And then I went over to Far Acre to check the ewes?"

"Ay."

"You know how Rachel's brother's been cutting her hedges."

"Ay. I know how Clarkson feels about that."

"Well, I was up on the bank after a ewe and happened to glance at the cottage. The back door was swinging in the wind."

"Swinging in the wind. What be the harm in that?"

"Well, nothing if everything else is well. But I got an uneasy feeling in my stomach. She's not an early riser."

"Granted."

"So that's what I'm saying. Her back door was open but her bedroom curtains were drawn."

"Well then. All you got to do is put your head in."

"I'll do that, soon as I get things straight here."

Nicolas looked out of Torridon's landing window and his eyes focused straight away on Rachel's blue Nissan. God dammit to hell, he thought; that blasted woman and her beastly little car. What the fuck was he to do about that?

While he brewed up a large cafetiere of coffee, he pondered his options. His immediate thought was that he must get rid of it. He would drive it to a cliff, release the hand brake, and jump out before he went with it, over the cliff and into the sea.

Fingerprints. He'd wipe them away.

Then what? Could he walk home from the south coast? That would be a stretch.

And what would be the outcome? The police would assume she'd committed suicide, but there'd be no body. Sometimes the sea did swallow people up, leaving no trace. Such things were occasionally reported on South West news.

On the other hand, they might suspect him of giving her and the car the push. The police could tell a lot from tyre marks and footprints. No, whatever solution he thought of would have to be watertight. It would have to fit a credible story.

What about leaving the Nissan in the nearest station car park? She'd run away with her fancy boy; they'd caught a train together. That was his best scenario. He'd have to do it at night and then walk home. He might be seen by someone who knew him, returning from the cinema. They'd offer him a lift. Delay the trip until after midnight. Better, perhaps, to tow it behind the Navara? What about CCTV cameras?

In the end, he decided the simplest course was the best. He'd leave it exactly where it was. He already knew how he'd field the questions that would eventually be asked.

Until then, he was fine. The coffee had made him feel good. He got himself and his things ready for the first trip of the day down the garden. My harem, he thought and that made him smile. He could feel his cheeks stretching with the unaccustomed exercise.

Robert was slowly waking from a dream, the sort of dream in which you can manipulate events. He'd been lying there, going over the few times he'd met Rachel. He started in Tina's studio, sitting on the old sofa with Tina's spaniel, Sam, at his feet. Lucy nudged him. "That's her," she said, leading him with her eyes to look towards a tall woman, leaning over a display of Tina's earthenware casseroles. She looked like the member of the women's hockey team he liked to watch. Long, lean, tanned legs in white shorts that came to her knees, a loose, dark-green sweat shirt that almost covered the shorts – it had a logo on it but he couldn't see what. Her straight fair hair hung forward, hiding her face. There was a strikingly bold streak of purple in the lock that curled under her chin. She looked exotic in the village setting. "That's Rachel Hines, you know, the artist?" Lucy described a story about a warthog. Robert was amused by the way she expected him to know the name of a children's book author. Rachel turned at that moment and caught his smile. She gazed at him intently and came across to the sofa. He felt abashed that she must have thought he was smiling at her. She perched on the arm of the sofa next to someone called Sally who was from London. They were friends.

He got to his feet. At this point, he put his arms around her small waist and pulled her into his embrace. No, he didn't do that. He took his waking dream back to the real happening. He offered her his place. To his surprise and chagrin, she walked away. It had taken a bare half a minute for Rachel to invade his mind. She'd been in occupation since then.

And here he was once more, going around and around, entangled with questions about her.

He could count on one hand the number of times they'd met. Each time they came across each other, he got the impression that she couldn't get away fast enough. Never before had he experienced this response from a woman. Usually, they were all over him. He took no particular pride in this; it was just the way things were. Yet the one woman he'd come across in the last few, barren years back in Devon, the single woman he actively wanted to attract, she was the one who appeared completely immune to him. It was her friend Sally that engineered the reason for meeting again, bouncy, exuberant Sally with her pink cheeks, big blue eyes and glossy, black hair. It was Sally who rang him and enquired about the progress of the Priory Cottage house sign, not Rachel. Perhaps he should push a little harder?

He could take her a jar of honey. He imagined knocking on her door, holding out the jar, People liked his honey. In his mind, he watched Rachel's face fall on seeing him. She closed the door. A wave of sadness washed through him. And this was just in his imagination!

What was it with Rachel? Her aloofness towards him made her even more tantalising. No wonder she featured in his dream life and occupied his daily thoughts so often.

"Good morning, Rachel," said Angela.

Rachel groaned by way of reply. She was sitting on the mattress. Her legs were drawn up and her elbows were propped on her knees. She held her head in her hands.

Angela took in her companion's appearance. Healthy - tanned – athletic – it made her feel ashamed of her own scrawny arms. "How are you feeling today? Head bad? You'd better let me look at your wound when we're up."

Rachel tried to turn her head away from Angela's attention. She could hear her neck creak.

"I know Nicolas won't want that cut going bad. I'll ask him to bring antiseptic."

As she spoke, Angela was conscious that her knuckles were barely healed from her last session on the rock wall. She tucked her hands under her arms. The downside of having a companion would be that she wouldn't be able to employ her usual tactics for deflecting panic and fear. Harming yourself is not a habit you can talk about with others. Still, she might not feel the need for that release, now she had a companion. She felt a sudden rush of energy. There was such a lot to ask; her questions were mounting. Had both the Johnsons died? They obviously had, otherwise Rachel wouldn't have bought the cottage. What price had she paid? Had she met Robert? Who else had she met? The Middletons, surely. What had she been doing in the priory ruins? Dreadful overgrown wilderness, dangerous piles of old stones, of no interest to man nor beast, although a few of the locals had been interested in doing something with them. Nicolas would have none of that. He wanted to keep everything as it was, of course. He was just like a Scottish laird, wanting to keep his thousand-acre grouse moors to himself. Same with his antique business. He bought things and kept them, untouched, never sold. Not much of a dealer's life in that. Now he had two living antiques to keep. On his track record as a hoarder, they should be safe.

"We've got to get out of here," said Rachel.

This was exactly what she feared. Her companion was not going to settle down, face reality, grin and bear it. She was a different type. She'd create trouble.

"What have you tried so far?" Rachel asked.

Tried! She certainly hadn't tried a thing. That was not the way to bring the imprisonment to an end. *Never provoke Nicholas*. She'd learnt that lesson well.

"The light flex for instance. We could pull the bulb fitting off the lead and yank the lead into the cell from wherever it comes from."

Angela regarded her with disbelief. Did she mean to *strangle* him?

"I suppose that is too long a shot. There'd be a plug or something on the end of it in the first cell."

Angela wanted to co-operate with Rachel, just so long as nothing came of it. "The lead comes into the cell from the workshop, I think. You could never pull it free."

Pathetic, thought Rachel. All this time sitting here and still not attempting to change the situation. She'd have to galvanize her into action, or else act for herself and leave Angela to her own devices. She would never be so hard, though.

She might be able to disarm Nicolas by using guile in some way. Trick him into lowering his defences, take him by surprise, seize the keys. She would study him and his routine.

She might spot an opportunity.

Meanwhile, people outside would be wondering where she was, if not yet, then very soon. Lucy would expect her to call. So would Sally. Betty Middleton might knock on her door, wanting her to go to Saturday market. There was Charlie at the pub. He sometimes phoned. The woman who made baskets wanted her to join one of her courses. A number of people were beginning to include her in various activities. She'd been asked to visit the primary school and talk about writing and illustrating the Walter books.

She felt better. It wouldn't be very long before she'd be discovered. Best to wait for that to happen than try anything physical on Nicolas. However strong she was, she would be no match for him. She wouldn't try her hand with the electric flex, and that was a relief. Coincidentally with that thought, the light came on.

"Oo, good, it's daytime!" Angela's voice was weak but full of cheer.

Rachel leant sideways so that Angela could remove her scrawny limbs from the bed and step over her and the mattress to a small, free section of the floor. In the light from the overhead bulb, the size of the cell she was sharing was once again evident. She judged it to be about the size of a modern garage on a housing estate where space is at a premium.

Angela used the bucket.

Behind Rachel's head, water dripped. She examined it carefully. It oozed down the rock wall from the ceiling and then was caught, drop by drop, in a slight depression, not deep enough to be thought of as a basin. The idea came to her that perhaps it came from Elfrida's healing spring. The thought filled her with hope.

Nicolas, with his mug of coffee in hand, stood at the kitchen window. It had been fine when he got up but now rain hammered against the glass. A strong north-westerly wind blew squalls of rain across the garden. The evergreen shrubs and young trees which he'd planted over the last few years bowed their heads towards the house, shaking their leaves before springing upright, only to be bowled over yet again. A day to stay indoors, but there was no hope of that. His two women would need attention at some point.

At least he didn't have to attend to the light. He'd installed a timer switch at the start, which was clever of him. It would be good if other chores could be seen to automatically. He imagined a food dispenser that could be filled once a week. He could make a tin box with seven compartments, set in the door between the inner and outer cell. The programmed mechanism would open one compartment a day in the cell, and a ready-meal would be delivered. He must watch that video again, the one about someone in a prison cell. There were useful tips to pick up from that.

Two women now, though. They'd take some feeding. Even as he dreamt it up, he knew his tin box idea was a non-starter.

He re-filled his mug. Probably the first thing he should do today was to go over to Priory Cottage. The sooner he set the scene in the cottage, the better. It wasn't dustbin day but the postman might need a signature or something. Also, Rachel had the occasional supermarket delivery. The bloody van men had no idea that other people used the parking. What if she'd ordered a delivery today? Or tomorrow? He'd have to take it in. Well then, more food would come in handy.

When the rain stopped half an hour later, he grabbed the chance to check on the cottage. First thing he found was the back door open and a pool of water on the tiled floor. He shut the door and looked at the sodden mat floating in a lagoon of water. This didn't fit in with the story he'd composed. Rachel – like Angela before her – had gone off with a man. Rachel's story was easier to make up, as she lived alone. He planned to find a suitcase and fill it with likely clothes. Nicolas heard himself saying to whoever enquired, "Oh, yes, I did notice someone turn up. Rachel got into his car with a suitcase. What colour car? Oh, I think it was grey, or was it blue? Sorry, I didn't pay much attention."

But here was water on the kitchen floor and a sodden mat. He'd have to deal with this. She wouldn't have gone away leaving the door open to let in the rain. If she'd shut and locked the door, there'd be no water on the floor. Sighing deeply, he set about finding the means to mop it up. First, he threw the mat outside. He found a bucket and sponge under the sink and set to work on his hands and knees. It took some time, sopping up the water in the sponge and squeezing it out in the bucket, then emptying the bucket in the sink and starting again. The level of water didn't go down as quickly as he expected. It had got under the kitchen unit by the door and a steady flow kept replenishing the pool. His back ached. Bloody Rachel fucking Hines, waltzing down to snoop in the ruins, leaving her bloody back door open. In the winter, too, when it was bound to rain. Having to be put in with Angela, into the bargain. Couldn't these bloody women leave a man in peace?

At last he'd mopped up well enough. Next: the upstairs jobs. He'd been inside and upstairs once before; the Johnsons had asked for his help with a heavy chest of drawers they wanted moving from one bedroom to the other. Now one of the two rooms had become Rachel's studio. He checked its appearance. Lots of things tacked to a cork wall. Pictures on a drawing board. Paintbrushes in a jar. He noted the view down her garden towards his workshop and the ruins beyond. Ideal position for spying on him. But no longer! The spy had been caught.

The next room was her bedroom. This is where he must set the scene. The bed was unmade, the pillow crumpled, the duvet flung aside. He thought of his mother and Angela who would never go away without leaving a room immaculate. How would Rachel compare with them? He decided she'd make half an effort, so he plumped up the pillow and fluffed up the duvet and made sure they were placed roughly in line with each other, the duvet slightly overlapping the pillow. He was pleased with the result. He picked up the striped pyjamas lying on the floor and stuffed them under the pillow. Next, he turned his attention to the clothes Rachel kept on open shelves. This was a more intimate task. It felt odd to be looking for the basic undergarments for Rachel to take away. She liked dark coloured and frilly underwear which sent a disturbing shiver through him. Skimpy pants, bras on the generous side. He hurried on, making a pile of suitable garments on the bed. Now he must find something to pack these things into. Where would Rachel keep luggage? He searched all the cupboards he could find in the cottage. How pokey it was. How did anyone live in such a small space? Torridon was only just big enough for him and he was a tidy man.

Eventually he found a two-wheeled flight bag in a cupboard under the stairs into which he stuffed the clothes he'd gathered. Then he sat down in the kitchen for a breather and a moment's thought. A pile of dirty dishes on the draining board caught his eye. For God's sake, woman! He'd even got to do her washing-up!

As he began to wash the plates, an insistent purring sound came from the windowsill above the sink. Rachel's cell phone! He looked at it with horror. Here was a problem. He'd have to get rid of it. He took the phone outside and jumped on it. It took several vigorous jumps before it was sufficiently smashed. Next, he'd have to get rid of the bits. He found a dustpan and brush and a freezer bag. He swept up the bits and emptied the pan into the bag. This would go into his own bin. He put the bag aside for the moment.

After he'd washed the plates and put them away carefully in places where they looked as if they belonged, he went back upstairs to check. Good lord, he'd nearly forgotten! Women always carry a handbag of some sort or other. Once again, he hunted all over the cottage but could only find an oversized, leather affair with a long strap and internal zip pockets which held a comb, a powder compact, car keys and a wallet. He added the contents of a bathroom shelf and the bits and pieces on her dressing table. God, if he'd overlooked all that…! He was now beginning to feel an edge of danger. He must keep his head.

The thing to do now was to pretend to be Rachel, leaving the cottage for a week or so. He went around the house checking windows. All shut and locked. In the living room, he looked thoughtfully at a pile of magazines and books. One was open, with her spectacles resting on the page. Book and specs went into the bag. He took a padded jacket from a hook in the hall.

It was a relief when, satisfied with his work, he locked the back door and left by the front, locking it behind him. He loped back to Torridon, keeping his head down – not that there was anyone for miles around to see him. How wise he was to live in an overgrown garden, at the end of a long track in the midst of fields.

Robert decided to call in on Lucy. It was after nine, which he knew was a good time for her. The little girls would have left for school, yet breakfast might still be on the table and he could join her for a second cup of coffee. She might have heard from Rachel. Tom was home from Abu Dhabi, too, and he needed to bring him up to date on the odd jobs he'd done around the place.

"Tom!" Lucy yelled up the stairs, baby on hip, kettle in hand. "Bob's here!"

"I don't want to wake him up, if he's still jet-lagged."

"No, he's fine. He'll be down in a minute. Coffee?"

"Please."

"Hold your godson a sec will you? What's the good of having a godfather next door if he does nothing to help."

"Steady on. Who spent three hours last week dealing with your overheating Aga?"

"Only teasing."

"I know. I'll forgive you."

Robert held out his arms for the baby. Six months old and grinning at him. Named after him, too, but known as Bobby. "Bob, bob, bobby, Bob!" chanted Robert, and the baby gurgled in a satisfactory way. Robert found everything about his next door neighbours enchanting. They'd become his family.

"I was wondering," he began, casually. He looked down at the baby, not at Lucy. "I was wondering," he repeated, "if you'd heard from Rachel."

Lucy turned from the sink where she was piling dishes. She smiled at him in a knowing kind of way.

Robert felt his face grow warm. "I was just wondering. I'm due to make her a house sign."

"I know."

"Have you heard from her?"

"No, but I don't expect to. Have you rung her cell phone? She may still be in London."

"No answer. Nor on her landline."

"Why don't you go over to her cottage and see if she's back."

"I don't think I could do that. She doesn't seem to like me very much."

"What makes you think that?"

"She seems to want to avoid me."

Lucy's brow and mouth puckered, in a half-frown, half-smile. "It may be for quite another reason," she said after a moment. "Tom and I came to the conclusion that she was under the impression you were my husband!"

"How on earth would she get that impression?"

"You know what village gossip can do. You do live next door. Tom is away a lot. You pop in regularly. I'm not surprised if she does think you and I are husband and wife."

Robert looked disturbed for a moment as he thought about this. Then his expression brightened. "If so, then that would explain why she's so distant with me. Do you think that could be the case?"

"I do. Something Sally said, too ... there was a married man she was with in London. She's been escaping him. She wouldn't want to fall for another."

A wave of optimism swept over Robert. "So you think - I might have some hope? If she understands I'm a crusty old bachelor?"

"I do! And I'll find out for certain when I next see her. Why not go over there and test our theory for yourself."

That was far too bold for him. "I'll wait a bit," he said.

"I'm worried about Rachel," Oliver told Matt over breakfast. "She doesn't answer her phone. I try her landline and her cell phone. Nothing. She could still be in London but she's not with Sally. I've called there. I'm just wondering whether she's gone back to Useless Martin."

"Oh dear me, if she has. Do you think she has?"

"It's possible. This has happened before. She makes up her mind to have nothing more to do with him and the next we know, they're thick as thieves again."

Matt let him ramble on for a while with his various worries. Then he suggested that Oliver drive to Priory Cottage and see for himself whether she was there or not. "She may be seeing Malcolm at weekends and not wanting you to know."

"That's all too possible. What an idiot she is."

Betty Middleton tapped out Rachel's number on her new Smartphone. She must make time for getting all her contacts transferred. Stan watched from across the table. He was a bit on the hot and bothered side today, with the wait to hear if Rachel was alright. He didn't like the way she lived on her own. Stan himself would have called round right away. He didn't trust Clarkson. Stan was one of the many who thought he'd done away with his wife. However, he had to leave it to Betty who knew best, and Betty said she didn't want Rachel to feel nannied. A phone call was the answer.

Betty found that Rachel's cell phone was dead. When she tried the landline, she was greeted by an answerphone message. When Betty went out, Stan dialled the number himself. He liked listening to her soft voice. *"This is Rachel Hines, I can't get to the phone right now, please leave a message."*

At the time, Rachel was voicing her curiosity about the drip. "I wonder if this has something to do with the healing spring."

Angela watched as she caught the next drop on a finger and tasted it.

"Mm, that's pure," said Rachel with surprise. "It doesn't taste of moss at all."

Angela said sourly that she couldn't imagine any kind of healing happening down here,

"On the contrary," said Rachel. "In Elfrida's day there was a spring which was thought to have healing powers. This wall must have been part of the original cave, the site of the spring, where Elfrida lived out her years as an anchorite."

What was Rachel on about? Angela let her burble on without feeling the need to engage in a conversation she couldn't follow. When eventually Rachel had said all she wanted to say, Angela drew her attention to the lines she'd scored in the greenstained rock. "See how the stain has grown? Here's the mark I made when I first thought of it. The second scratch I made some time later. This latest one was after a really long time. I'd say it's spread about three millimetres since I started checking."

Sometime ago … a really long time … Angela was a hopeless

sort of person. Rachel would have been marking days right from the start of her imprisonment. In fact, she should do that right away, just in case she'd be here for longer than a day or two. Being here as long as Angela was beyond the realms of possibility. "What do you use? To mark the wall?"

Angela ran her hand over the cement brick wall that held the door. "Oh bless me, I can't have lost it!"

Yes, she was completely hopeless, thought Rachel.

"No, correction! I've got it." Angela held a small shard of stone in her hand. It looked like one of those flints shaped by Neolithic people to cut and clean hides.

"Oh well done!" Rachel had realised, in the few short hours they'd spent together, what a lot of encouragement Angela needed. She was a person lacking in any vestige of self-esteem. The poor woman, cowed into submission by Clarkson! Ever since she'd met the man, she'd been aware - and wary - of his power. Passive aggression in spades, she thought. But then – going at him with a knife! Angela had found her inner warrior, without doubt. Just a shame that the two of them hadn't been able to find the balance in themselves and between each other.

Come to think of it, who was she to know better? She, in her own way, had submitted to the rules laid down by Martin. It had taken her years to break free.

She took the stone from Angela and made two marks on the wall above the drip. "Day One done. Day Two just begun." Although she was held prisoner, she would do everything in her power to make her sentence short.

Nicolas stared at the contents of Rachel's flight bag which he'd emptied onto the large mahogany table in Torridon's sombre dining room. The last time the room had been used was when they'd had the Johnson couple to a meal, an occasion which Angela had organised very much against his will. He shuffled garments around the table without purpose while thoughts and scenes from the past tumbled over each other in his mind. He'd spoilt Angela. She often made out that he never let her do anything and that was blatantly untrue. He'd spent his life devoted to her well-being. She could make any number of friends, as far as he was concerned. Ruth Johnson was pretty well the only local person who she spent any time with and he never stopped her. If she was lonely, that was her fault. He pulled garments to and fro while his thoughts ran on. She could take up squash, too, but did she? No. She was not like him, the outgoing type. He had friends he met at the club and sometimes in Charlie's pub. There was nothing to stop her doing the same. You can't blame someone else for your own wimpishness. But all that was years ago, part of his life *Before*. Now it was *After*. He might even have to think of this period under a new name. It had taken a radical new shape. Now it wasn't just *After* Angela's onset of madness and the start of her life in the cell, it was now after that first after. He'd think of this new period as *Double After*.

Double trouble.

He stared at Rachel's clothes, trying to work out what she'd take away with her. He'd probably taken far too many things from her bedroom shelves for his story to convince a policeman if – god forbid – the situation unravelled. He wasn't sure what women wore. He never noticed. Angela was no guide. She had a pair of jeans, a track suit and a couple of grey sweat shirts which, like her underclothes, alternated between being worn and washed. The washed half of the cycle was always coming around but maybe it wasn't more than once a month. With the moon, he thought with a wry smile. But that lay in the past. Be thankful for small blessings, he told himself; she'd at last passed the age of needing him to shop for *items of feminine hygiene*. But now, with Rachel on the scene--- his heart sank. She was young enough. He'd be back on that ghastly task. What a dismal turn his life had taken. Bloody women.

He stuffed into a carrier bag half the pile of clothes which he'd distribute among Exeter's charity shops, a little at a time. He returned the rest to the flight bag which he'd take to the cell for Rachel's use. There was now only the shoulder bag to deal with. That would go to the cell too. After all, it was the safest place to hide things.

With a deep sigh at the extent of his worries, he turned his attention to food.

"What time will Nicolas turn up today? Does he bring breakfast?"

Angela gave a short burst of laughter. "Are you imagining croissants? Well-brewed coffee? *Marmalade?*"

Rachel apologised for being so naïve. Hearing the imaginary menu made her stomach rumble. She clutched it.

Angela felt immediately sorry for her. "I know what a shock this must be for you. I promise – you will get used to it. I always tell myself that things could be much worse. I could *really* be in prison."

"But that's not possible. Unless of course you've done something criminal."

Angela was on the verge of telling Rachel the details of the knife incident but drew back. That would come out when they knew each other better. Meanwhile, she filled her in on what to expect. Nicolas could turn up at any time before dark, but his usual time was around the middle of the day as far as it was possible to judge. They would hear him unlocking the outer door, bringing things in – it could take him a while, crashing about – they'd hear the door thud shut and being locked and bolted. Then their door would be opened and Nicolas would appear with their food and water. He'd go in and out for a while, taking out the bucket, replacing it with a clean one, bringing in a thermos of tea or coffee and a plastic freezer container of whatever food he'd managed to put together. Sometimes it was savoury, other times sweet, but never both on the same day. Bread would be included without fail. Potatoes seldom. Rice was a rarity. Spaghetti bolognese, frequent. Tinned, of course. If it was a curry, it would be left-overs from his own take-away meal. He did his best, she told Rachel. "You won't starve."

Rachel looked at Angela skinny frame. If she stayed here any length of time, she'd soon look like Angela. But she was going to be out of the cell well before she reached starvation point.

"Coo-ee! Hello! Mr Clarkson! Nicolas!"

Nicolas was wheeling the flight bag down the garden, the basket of food in his free hand and Rachel's shoulder bag hanging at his side. He came to a halt, his heart giving a series of sickening thuds in his chest as he heard his name being called.

Betty Middleton was approaching around the side of the house. "Oh, I'm glad I've caught you. I'm a trifle concerned about Rachel."

Nicolas's brain was working fast, although he didn't move. He *couldn't* move. The worst had happened. Goddammit, he couldn't even go about his daily business without that bloody Betty Middleton poking her nose in. He needed to think of a reason for what he was carrying down the garden.

"You see, I noticed yesterday her back door was open and her curtains drawn so I've been calling her all morning and just getting her answerphone. So I came round. Stan said that was best. And the back door's shut now and the curtains drawn back, so she's been up and about, but I got no answer at the front, nor at the back, and there's a sopping wet doormat cast out all anyhow which is not like her a bit, she's such a neat person even if she is tall."

Nicolas felt a flash of irritation at Betty's lack of logic but he musn't let himself be distracted. His main concern was how to explain his present position, halfway down his garden with a flight bag, a woman's shoulder bag, and a basket with a thermos sticking upright among plastic containers of food. Betty's gimlet eyes would be taking it all in.

"I don't mean to pry," said Betty, stopping in her tracks. She was unnerved by Nicolas's silence. He hadn't even turned.

"I was just wondering," she went on, "if you'd seen her lately. I know she was away in London but I thought she'd be home by now."

Nicolas grabbed at this. "I haven't seen her. I thought she was still in London."

"Well then, that must be it. Sorry to disturb you."

He gathered himself together and turned towards Betty with a smile. He must be civil. "Not at all," he managed. "You're right to be concerned. You never know these days. I'll let you know if I see her. Learn anything." Now he was going too far.

However, it seemed to satisfy Betty because she turned tail and disappeared around the house, making for the front gate. He waited until he heard her start her car and drive away. He continued to the workshop, aware of the annoying tremble in his hands. Another bloody woman.

"Stan. Did you hear what I said?"

"Eh?" Stan was pouring water into the kettle. "What was that?"

"Nicolas had a flight bag."

"He's going on holiday then?"

Betty hadn't thought of this explanation. All the same, it didn't fit in with what she'd seen. She described the scene in more detail. "And he went bright red in the face," she ended, by way of a finale. "As if I'd caught him shoplifting."

Stan put the kettle on the stove. "Well, he is a bloody funny bugger, agreed."

"But taking a flight bag and a thermos to his workshop!"

"I don't see nothing wrong with that. I expect he had a

whole lot of antiques with him and wanted hot tea for his elevenses." He sat down at the kitchen table while he waited for the kettle to boil. Elevenses with Betty was a mid-morning pleasure. "What's more important," he went on, "is Rachel. Did you see her?"

"No, but she has been back. Everything looked normal except for her doormat. Left outside in the rain. Sopping wet. Why do you think she'd leave the doormat outside to get rained on?"

"Search me," said Stan.

Rachel and Angela heard the sounds of Nicolas's entry into the outer cell: the clank of bolts, the creak of the door being opened and almost immediately shut, these were easy to interpret. Other sounds that penetrated into their cell were so faint their source could only be guessed at. Angry swearing and unidentifiable thumps were followed at last by the welcome sound of their own door being unbolted and unlocked.

Rachel was ready with her strategy. "Good morning, Nicolas," she said brightly. "What's it like outside today? Still raining?"

Nicolas stood in the doorway holding a tray with both hands. There was no floor space. He could only enter if he stood on her mattress. She watched his face as he responded to her; first, surprise followed by bafflement. He clearly wasn't expecting a civil approach. She went on fast, "Can I help you in any way?"

If you could see a thunderstorm approaching on a human face, you could see it now. Her carefully thought-out approach might not be the right one. Angela evidently thought Rachel was courting trouble. She was sitting on her bed, hugging her knees, watching the developing scene apprehensively from behind a matted fringe of greyish-fair hair.

Nicolas kicked at the mattress.

"I was thinking," said Rachel, "wouldn't it be better if I

slept in the other room." Not a question, more a statement. Room, not cell. All part of her chosen approach. She took hold of the corners of the mattress nearest to her and began to roll it towards the door. It was a sluggish weight but she was determined. Nicolas could do nothing but back away. She and the mattress followed him into the outer cell.

She arranged the mattress to one side of the much bigger space. Her flight bag caught her eyes. "Oh, how kind! You've brought my overnight things! I'll be able to have a good wash."

Nicolas, backed against the further door, still held the tray: hunks of bread and two cups of hot tea. "Wash! Water's in short supply, I'd have you know."

"I only need a little. And I'll have a shower when I get home."

"Home! You won't be going home. That's something I can't allow, you must see that."

"On the contrary," said Rachel in the sort of tone she'd used with Walter's publicity department staff: calm and logical, taking agreement for granted. "All my friends will be wondering where I am today. I have various things arranged. If I don't turn up, they'll be on to the police straight away."

Her words did not match her view of the situation but she spoke with conviction. She could tell Nicolas was unnerved. He was dithering around the cell, not knowing where to put down the tray while he muttered about getting the mattress back to its right place, in with Angela.

Meanwhile, Angela had tiptoed towards the open door between the two cells, following the exit of Nicolas, Rachel and the mattress. She was gazing up at the grille. She could see a strip of sky. She took a deep breath and closed her eyes to savour the dream.

Later on in the day, she and Rachel lounged on the mattress in the outer cell, idly chatting while they drank a second mug of tea. However hard she tried and however carefully she went over the events of the day, she could not understand how Rachel had managed to make such a huge difference to her life in just 24 hours. Somehow or other she had Nicolas running around on errands. "Bless me," she thought, "he might even let us out one day!"

DAY THREE

Neither of them had ever before enjoyed the luxury of an honest and meandering conversation with a single, compatible and amenable companion, with no interruptions or time limits imposed by anyone else. As Angela watched Rachel marking the third day on the rock wall, she remarked on this. "I know it's a dreadful cliché," she said, "but I feel I've known you for ever."

"Same here!"

"Your company – well, it's made me realise I've been lonely all my life."

"So have I," said Rachel. "Been lonely, that is. And yes, sharing this tiny space and our talks – that's made me see it."

"Hard to believe, though, in your case. Your life has been full of people. Not like mine."

"Lots of people, true, but I've never spent this kind of time with just one person. I don't think I've ever been really happy." Did she mean that? She'd startled herself. "Malcolm and I never lived together. I used to think I valued my independence. Now I think I'd like to be married." If she had a partner or husband, in fact any sort of companion, waiting for her in Priory Cottage, then she'd have been rescued by now.

Angela, thinking of her own married life, made a harrumph sound.

Rachel murmured her understanding. "Yes, I know. It depends who it is. You and Nicolas – it must have been difficult."

"Yes."

"What made you choose him in the first place?"

"Stupidity." In the old days she used to run her hand through her hair in moments of puzzled thought. It was a habitual gesture which she'd become aware of now that her fingers got stuck in tangles.

"Itchy?" asked Rachel, nervously thinking of fleas.

"Nicolas doesn't understand hair. He says it doesn't matter what I look like. Well, that's true enough in here. But it's the *feel* of it. He has so little hair himself and the little he has he keeps shaved. It's hard enough to get him to provide enough warm water for me to wash properly. Now he'll have to bring it for you, too. Enough for a shampoo – well, that's not going to happen. I have to make do with dry shampoo in little packets. You wait and see."

"I'm not waiting to see anything. We'll get out of this. Look around you. See how easy it was to get him to let us have the run of both chambers. One door open, only one to go!"

Angela was amazed by Rachel's optimism. She seemed to think that she could manipulate Nicolas. Some hope! More likely, her friends would be raising the alarm. "Who do you know around here? Who's going to be worried about you?"

Rachel thought hard. Sally in London? No. Their friendship didn't demand constant contact and they'd recently been together. Besides, it was time for Sally's annual skiing holiday. Lucy? No. The last time they'd met she'd told Lucy that she didn't need another sketching session. Betty Middleton? Possibly. "Betty and Stan," she suggested aloud.

Angela agreed. "They used to keep an eye out for me, too. Like the Johnsons. But no-one could have been really bothered when I disappeared. Otherwise, I wouldn't still be here. Were you told anything about me?"

"Lots of colourful stories. You'd been murdered. Or you went off with another man. I believe you were officially registered by the police as a Missing Person."

"Oo, was I." Angela smiled. Registered missing! She felt she'd gained some sort of qualification. No one thought her dead. That was an encouraging piece of news. "I expect it was Robert who notified the police."

Rachel put aside her mug carefully. Robert. Would he notify the police about her own disappearance? She wished she had been friendlier towards him. "Oh, Bob." She kept her voice casual. "Was he a friend of yours?"

"Yes. I met him through the Johnsons. He's a relation of some sort. Or was, I should say, now Lionel and Ruth have died. He was often at the cottage, helping them with various things. You've met him then? I liked him a lot."

With Rachel's encouragement, she went on to explain about Bob, who'd sold his family farmhouse to Tom and Lucy. He'd taken up blacksmithing when he retired from banking. He'd had some sort of breakdown. Too much stress in the City.

Rachel listened intently but she was finding it hard to take in the import of what Angela was telling her. It was time to get a grip on this.

"Did you say Lucy and *Tom*?" she asked. "Who on earth is Tom?"

"Lucy's husband."

Angela was surprised by Rachel's expression. She looked as if she'd been struck in the midriff by a sandbag. "What did you think?" she asked, but she didn't wait for an answer. She wanted to get back to Robert's history which Rachel hadn't seemed to take in. She elaborated. "When his parents died, he sold the farmhouse to Tom and Lucy but kept the milking parlour. So when he had his mini breakdown…"

"Just a second, Angela. Isn't *Robert* Lucy's husband?" She needed to have it spelt out clearly.

"Heavens, no!" Angela laughed at the thought. Robert was a dyed-in-the-wool bachelor. She was glad he'd always stayed single. It made it easier to fantasise about him, which she did on a regular basis, especially since being holed up here. She suspected, from Rachel's expression, that she, too, had fallen for Robert. Who wouldn't. He had let down the Johnsons, true. They'd lost quite a bit of money through his advice. But that mishap had come about through his keenness to help them. There was no need to tell Rachel about that side of things.

She went on, "Tom and Lucy were married before they

moved here and bought the farmhouse. Bob's just their daytime neighbour., when he's working in the forge. He lives in the village. As Tom is in oil, he's away for long periods. Bob does odd jobs for Lucy. They're good friends, nothing more." Or so it suited her to think.

"I thought …" began Rachel, but decided not to continue. She needed a quiet time to understand fully that she'd been mistaken. Robert was a single man, whose daytime work took place next door to Tom and Lucy's home. It was simple, really. She'd been foolish, leaping to conclusions. As a result, she'd put off the one person who could be her saviour. *Blast it!*

Sally rang Robert. "Have you seen Rachel at all?"

"No. I thought she must still be with you in London."

"No. She left some time ago. I can't raise her on her landline or her cell phone. I was wondering if you might go around to the cottage, just to check? I'm about to go off on holiday."

Robert hesitated. Lucy had suggested that Rachel's assumption he was her husband was the reason for her distant manner, But he wasn't confident. He still thought Rachel wouldn't like him to call round. What reason would he give for not visiting her? If he attempted to explain the subtle coolness that she maintained towards him, Sally was the sort of person who'd want to put things right. She'd make more of it than there was. As things stood, there was nothing that could be pinned down, explained or healed. He remembered something else Lucy had mentioned. "Wasn't there going to be a book fair in Germany? Or was it Italy? Perhaps she's gone to that."

"Bologna," supplied Sally. "She went last year. It could be early this year. Yes, she might well be there. She has a new project." She relaxed. That was the explanation for Rachel's silence. She wouldn't worry about her. She was likely having a high old time. So would she. *Val d'Isere, here I come*, she thought happily.

Tina rang Robert.

"Have you seen Rachel lately?"

"No, actually, I haven't. Why do you ask?"

"She was going to commission some mugs. She has an idea, something to do with the priory's Elfrida legend. She was going to fix a date to come to the studio to talk about it."

"That sounds like her new project. Sally thinks she's in Italy, trying to sell the idea."

Sandy, the local antiquarian book dealer, rang Tina.

"I'm having trouble getting in touch with Rachel. Her cell phone number doesn't work and she doesn't respond to her landline. She ordered a book and it's come in. Do you know if she's away?"

"She's in Italy," replied Tina.

Rachel's flight bag stood in a corner of the outer chamber, her shoulder bag leaning against it. The two women had been more intent on learning about each other than bothering to see what the bags contained. Rachel hadn't thought it worth unpacking as she'd be out of here in no time flat. It was Angela who'd become keen for Rachel to open the bags.

"See if he put in shampoo." Anticipation made it feel like a childhood Christmas.

Rachel emptied the contents of both bags onto her mattress. Bras, pants, sweatshirts, jogging trousers – brush, comb, deodorant, shampoo! If Nicolas brought them enough really hot water, they could both wash themselves properly and share out the clothes between them.

Angela's elation lasted until Nicolas arrived with the container of cold water. He did not respond well to Rachel's request for two buckets of hot water.

"You think this is a hotel? My god, woman, you bloody well put up with what I give you. You brought this on yourself. I didn't invite you here. Think about it!"

He stumped through to the inner cell to replace the full loo bucket with an empty one. Angela and Rachel, sitting together on the mattress among the clothes and oddments, exchanged glances as they heard him swearing.

"Poor Nicolas," whispered Angela with a smile that mixed amusement with sympathy.

Rachel took note of her expression. She could have been a mother proud of a son's difficult behaviour. That was the way Angela had got through years of life with Nicolas. She was willing to put up with anything, for the sake of peace and quiet.

Rachel, though, was not going to give up on her own strategy. When Nicolas came back in to the outer cell with the lidded bucket, she got to her feet. "Let me help you," she said. She held the bucket while he unbolted and unlocked the door to the outside; then she handed him the bucket, which he put down on the grass, before closing and locking the door on her.

She turned to Angela. "You see? We could overpower him another time. It's just a matter of having a plan ready."

Angela felt an inner quaking. Overpower Nicolas! He could go mad with rage, without her saying or doing a thing. She'd seen it happen a dozen times, and suffered for it. She'd have to change Rachel's attitude, for their own well-being.

The door creaked open and Nicolas came back in with the usual plastic container of food in a basket.

"Thank you so much," said Rachel. "for doing that rather unpleasant job."

"That's right!" barked Nicolas. "*Thank you.*" He leant over Angela and shook her shoulder. "Hear that? That's what you should be saying to me. Learn from your friend!"

"We're both grateful," Rachel said in her light, measured tones. "Angela has been telling me how kind you've always been to her."

Nicolas and Angela regarded her with blank amazement.

"Yes, it hasn't been easy for either of you. But then, that's how it's had to be."

They each bore the trace of a frown on their faces, as they worked out how Rachel's words could possibly match their personal experience.

"So I reckon," went on Rachel, "we have to work out ways to make it easier for you."

For a second, Angela thought that Rachel was going to suggest something outrageous like running back and forth between Torridon and the cell carrying their own food.

"Like what, may I ask?" said Nicolas in his sarcastic voice.

"We could cook in here," said Rachel. "Bring us a camping gas stove."

Nicolas said nothing and left them to discover what food the basket contained today. He had made an effort and included two apples. As he locked and bolted the door behind him, he imagined Rachel biting into her apple. She'd be even more grateful.

The apples were windfalls with puckered skin and soft, yellowish brown patches. Angela found them a familiar sight. "They'll have been stored in Torridon's cellar since the autumn," she told Rachel. "He can't bear to throw anything away."

"I can't work out if that's good or bad for us. He'll want to keep us until we're as old and withered as these apples?"

Angela liked the way Rachel could make her smile. "That should be good for us, then," she said. "Better than chucking out our dead bodies!"

"Oh, Angela, don't even joke." She gave an involuntary shudder. "We're getting out on our own two legs, alive and well, very soon. I promise you." She turned her attention to the book that Nicolas had – surprisingly – included in the shoulder bag: Hermits and Anchorites of Medieval England. She'd bought it before Christmas from Sandy, the secondhand book dealer. Nicolas had even included her reading glasses. For a moment, she thought of him as a kind and thoughtful man, which was absurd given her present situation as his captive. The book fell open at the page she'd been reading before she'd clambered into Torridon's territory to investigate the priory ruins. She felt the medieval world lay almost tangibly close. The 13th century occupant of this very place seemed to be within reach, standing beside her. Elfrida had chosen to live out her life here. Died here, too. Rachel remembered reading in the Johnsons' notebook that the anchorite had slept in a shallow depression in the floor of a cave. This was to be her eventual grave. The two chambered cell where she and Angela were incarcerated might have modern cement blocks in its walls but she was sure that it was formed from the remains of Elfrida's anchorage within the priory ruins. She had spent her first night on the floor of the inner cell, maybe on the very spot where Elfrida had slept and died. A hand seemed to creep around her heart, to comfort or to frighten her rigid, it was hard to tell.

To anchor herself back in the present she turned to Angela who had found Rachel's gold-coloured compact of pressed powder and foundation. She held it up close to her eyes and was peering at her reflection in the lid's mirror.

"Oh bless me! Do I really - ? I can't believe it. Do I really look such a freak? No wonder you screamed at me!"

Rachel suggested that she could give Angela's hair a good comb.

She held in her mind the image of the tresses she would draw for Elfrida, modelled on Lucy's abundance of blonde, wavy locks, as she tentatively brought her comb to engage with Angela's grey tangles. After a while of increasingly robust pulling, she gave up. "I tell you what. I'll ask Nicolas to bring scissors. You won't mind, will you, getting rid of it? You'll look good, especially when we can boil up water on the camping gaz for a good shampoo."

Angela regarded her with round, blue eyes, full of admiration and doubt. She didn't see any reason why Rachel shouldn't *ask* but Nicolas would never allow scissors within a mile of her.

DAY FOUR

Angela sat on the chair in the inner cell, one of Rachel's sweat shirts around her shoulders. She held the open compact in front of her face and watched in its mirror as Rachel cut handfuls of hair from her head.

"Is that just a bit too much?" she asked anxiously every now and again.

Rachel was intent on cutting away the impenetrable tangles. "You'll look fantastic," she told Angela. She wasn't quite as confident about this as she sounded. Her mind turned to images of Parisian girls at the end of world war two, being paraded through the street with shorn heads. It was as though Angela was being punished for a crime she hadn't committed. Yet what was that thing she'd told her about knives? Angela had run at Nicolas with a knife, which was why he'd incarcerated her. In spite of that story, Nicolas had brought a pair of sharp scissors to the cell at her request, without demur. He did have a kind streak within him. She was full of hope that she'd eventually persuade him to let them go. One little step at a time.

Today's step was actually a giant one. Besides the sharply pointed sewing shears from Angela's needlework basket, Nicolas had also brought them a camping gas stove and a large saucepan. Rachel was almost as amazed by this success as Angela was. They each thanked him profusely. He looked momentarily and pleasantly taken aback at receiving such gratitude. All the same, he removed the loo bucket with his usual spate of angry swearing.

By the time of lights out they'd both washed their hair and themselves in a series of basins full of water heated to just the right temperature on the camping gas. Then they'd cooked up some spaghetti. No sauce but hey, who minded. "Bliss," said Angela. Rachel scratched a cross beside the mark for Day Four to register the triumph.

DAY FIVE

"Bless me," said Angela, looking aghast at her reflection in the compact's mirror. Light coming through the grille showed her the extraordinary sight of a woman with a halo of short, prickly hair. "I look like a hedgehog!"

Rachel laughed at this. "You don't, not in the least. You look elegant."

"Elegant! Not in a hundred years would I ever look elegant. Especially not down here."

"You have very good bone structure. Your skull is a beautiful shape."

"Oh, shut up." Angela didn't like to think of skulls.

"If Nicolas would bring my sketch pad and pencils, I'd draw you."

Angela thought Rachel was being absurd. For the first time in the last four days, her usual feeling of hopelessness hit her. Alright, so Rachel had got Nicolas bending over backwards to please her, but there was a limit beyond which he would not go. That limit would be coming very soon and then where would they be? Back to where she'd been for the last however many years. It might have been better if she'd never been joined by Rachel.

She pulled herself together at this thought. Rachel's presence was a gift. "I don't know what you'd draw, except a cartoon."

Rachel laughed again.

"Bless me, please don't think I'm not grateful. My hair feels gorgeous even if I do look like someone being electrocuted."

Rachel was growing to like Angela's dry humour, which was a surprise coming from someone so – what exactly was she? Pious? Meek? Good?

Later in the long, dark day, Rachel heard Angela's *bless me* yet again and this time it provoked her into commenting. "Who are you asking to bless you? I'm intrigued."

Angela was surprised. "I don't think I've ever thought about it. It's just something I say, or always said, more likely. A habit from my rectory childhood? I suppose I'm asking God to bless me. Actually, it was my mother, not my dad, who used to exclaim *Bless me*, now I come to think of it."

"And you carry on. Do you believe in God then?"

"Oh heavens," said Angela with a smile. "now you're asking."

"This place must be absolutely thick with prayers to God."

Angela looked puzzled. "Why on earth?" It didn't feel to her a bit like a holy place, even if it was in the priory ruins behind Nicolas's workshop.

"You must know the legend!"

"I'm not sure that I do."

"The priory legend about the nun? How could you have lived in Torridon and not heard about Elfrida?"

"Oh, now you come to mention it, I do remember hearing about someone with a name like that. A recluse, way back in the Middle Ages? That was more to do with Nicolas. There were local meetings about the ruins, I think. He didn't want me to take part. Generally, he kept me away from other people. I don't know what he expected me to do. Grab hold of them and promise my undying love for them."

"Well, that's what Sir William Delamere did to Elfrida. They were betrothed. Then he raped her and she turned to Christ and a life of prayer."

"Is that the legend?"

"Yes, and she spent her life right here. She was only 14 when it happened."

"Bless me!"

"Bless her!"

"Oh how horrid."

"I'm thinking of writing about it."

"A Rachel Hines children's book?" Angela was impressed by Rachel's history, which had come out during their long conversations. "Illustrated too? That would be marvellous!"

"Not a children's book. Not with a rape. I don't know how I could give reason enough for Elfrida to become an anchorite without a really dramatic reason for escaping from the world. Saying that, though, makes me realise that lots of people in the middle ages did become hermits and anchorites. It was an alternative to a life of hardship and poverty. In the cell they were supported. They had food and shelter, the basics."

"Yes, I saw the book Nicolas brought you."

"Hellfire was completely real for them. They could see ghastly things painted on church walls. That's what awaited them if they didn't recant their sins. Flames licking at their ankles. Being consumed by eternal fire. Just imagine!"

"No thank you, I'd rather not. There's purgatory, too. As a child, I believed in purgatory as well as hell, both the stages I'd have to go through unless I repented of my sins. I never understood what sins I might have committed. I still don't know but I reckon I've been in purgatory for the last few years. And hell before that!"

"It was a man's world. Still is. I've been thinking about all this during our long, black nights in Elfrida's cell. Men need women to be two things: Virgin mother and prostitute. Impossible to find both present in a single individual. The Bible was written by men. They made the rules. They told the story we were, still are, expected to live by. We were an afterthought, made from Adam's rib. I ask you! The apple of knowledge? Eve's fault we were thrown out of the Garden of Eden. Don't let women be clever, get educated. That held true well into the 20th century – still holds true in some parts of the world. Don't pay them the same wage as men for the same job, otherwise they'll start bossing us men around. Men need to hold onto power, so that they can do what they like with us."

Angela looked glum. "Surely that's not still true?"

"Look where we are. This is just the extreme end of the spectrum of power."

Rachel wanted to cheer her up. She told her that, if she liked, she would tell her the story of Elfrida as she had so far made it up in her mind. Angela nodded enthusiastically.

"Let's get comfortable, then." They lay down on the mattress in the outer chamber and pulled Rachel's duvet up to their chins. "Right. Here goes," said Rachel. Angela folded her arms across her ribs and closed her eyes. This was the way to spend a day.

Nicolas put his bags of supplies on the ground in front of the cell's outer door and brought the largest key to the centre of the key ring hanging on the chain from his belt. At least it wasn't raining today, for the first time for weeks. It would soon be spring. Intermittent birdsong came from the willows behind the hillock in which the cell's heavy oak entrance door was set. He'd always wanted to use this marvellous door and its twin, found years ago in a treasure trove of a reclamation yard. They were probably Victorian copies of Tudor originals, worth twice or three times his original outlay. He'd certainly never foreseen this, their eventual and perfect use.

The lift in his spirits vanished as he entered the first chamber. It felt dank and smelt bad. Depression clamped down on his innermost being. The burden of responsibility for the lives of two women was not what he had foreseen or planned for. Thoughts of a possible solution returned to his mind. He could so easily stir rat poison into their soup, spice it up with curry so they wouldn't notice, and that would be the end of his problems. He could lock the cell on them and leave. No-one had found Angela. He'd been safe for the last three and a half years. He'd be able to enjoy his life again once he freed himself from the never-ending tasks of caretaker.

But rat poison? That would give them an agonising death. He banished the visions that sprang to mind. He was not cruel. Far better to simply lock the door on the problem and leave. That would be kinder. No. Not kind at all. Death by starvation and dehydration was unlikely to be comfortable. He could give them a bottle of whisky and lots of sleeping pills? No. They wouldn't take them. The life force was strong. They'd go on waiting for rescue as Angela had done for years, and now Rachel, too. Bloody women! Why were they such a problem?

He knew perfectly well that his thinking was somehow disturbed – he was stressed after all - but that knowledge came and went fleetingly in only one corner of his mind, like the tide in a hidden cove. He had to concentrate all his mental powers on immediate, practical concerns.

Taking several journeys, he brought all the necessary gear into the first chamber– the containers of water and the bags of supplies shopped in Exeter with such difficulty. Next, he locked and barred the outer door behind him, Then he unlocked the inner door.

The eyes of the two women were fixed on him as he entered.

"Shampoo?" asked Rachel.

"Brush? Comb?" Angela's comb had snapped in Rachel's hands when she was dealing with the tangles before the radical cut. Now she was enjoying her new hair style. Every now and again she would check her appearance in Rachel's compact's mirror, tilting her head this way and that. Perhaps she really did have good bone structure!

"Wait for it, wait for it." Hadn't that been a catchphrase at one point? Nicolas felt jovial. Sure enough, the continual chores were boring but there was pleasure, too, in being the provider, thanked and praised for the care he gave.

DAY SIX *or seven or eight*

Robert was working on Rachel's cottage sign, even though she hadn't yet agreed a design. Hammering out shapes in hot iron always soothed him. It was particularly necessary to be soothed nowadays. Ever since Lucy had suggested a reason for Rachel's coolness, he'd turned this over in his mind as a possibility. If Lucy was right, then Rachel must have the situation clarified as soon as possible. There was no reason why he couldn't call round and tell her that he was single. But how would he put it? It sounded too bald. He waited for Lucy to make it plain, on his behalf. Then he changed his mind once more. He couldn't wait. He needed to see and tell Rachel. Tap, tap, hammer, hammer. He could not let her remain ignorant. He could not let her slip away from him, through a misunderstanding.

What he could do, he realised, was to get in touch with Rachel's brother Oliver. They'd met at the cottage. Oliver had given him his number, saying he was welcome to visit him in Exeter.

He rang at once. Oliver responded straight away. He hadn't been able to raise Rachel either. They arranged to meet on Saturday at Priory Cottage, agreeing that Rachel musn't feel that they'd been worried about her or that she was being checked up on. *You're nannying me*; that was the sort of thing Oliver guessed she'd say. Robert suggested that their excuse for meeting at the cottage was a mutual interest in the priory ruins. Oliver suggested saying that they liked each other's company and had met several times over the winter.

"Without her knowing? Will she believe that?" asked Robert doubtfully.

"Oh, certainly she will. I make friends easily. She and I both."

Robert felt full of hope; then immediately worried that Rachel would think him gay. He'd have to make sure she wouldn't leap to the wrong conclusion.

Nicolas had successfully unloaded a bag in an Exeter charity shop, one of several such shops earmarked to receive small portions of Rachel's clothes and shoes – the parts of her wardrobe that she would take away with her in the winter, for a good long stay abroad with a lover. So far he hadn't had the story tested. No-one had turned up looking for her. He'd been lucky.

Lucky in one respect. Unlucky in others. He was in Boots filling a wire basket with Rachel's demands. Toothpaste! Face cream! Shampoo! Deodorant! *Items of feminine hygiene!* Angela had never asked for so many different things, with such insistence on different brands. How was it that he was meekly carrying out Rachel's wishes? "Beats me," he said to himself. A nearby shopper looked at him askance. He must have spoken aloud. His arm shot out to add innocuous items to his basket, to hide the embarrassing packets. When it was full, he went to a corner by the weighing machine and transferred the contents to his shopping bag. Bloody women! He walked out.

A few yards down the street, he felt his arm gripped. A large woman with a heavily made-up face was asking him something. After a moment, he understood that he'd inadvertently missed going to a till and paying. He went back inside the shop, explaining how stressed he was, with his sick wife at home, likely to die any minute.

He barely knew what he said, he was so shaken. Driving home, he recalled his words. Perhaps he'd actually voiced the truth. Would he soon have to bring about Angela's and Rachel's demise? It might well come to that. Poison would be the kindest way. He'd better look into ways and means. He must be prepared. There could be a crisis and he'd have to take immediate action.

One thing had become clear. It had been fine when it had just been Angela to look after. Having two women to care for was an entirely different kettle of fish, especially as one of them was the kind of woman he'd never come across before. She was a witch.

Later, arriving home, he was disturbed to see two cars in the parking space, besides Rachel's blue Nissan. What the hell? Was his story about to be challenged? He pulled himself together, reminding himself of his script. He pulled up by his barn and went in through the gate to join two men. They were resting against the bonnet of Rachel's car, looking away from him. They turned as the scrunch of gravel announced his approach.

"Good afternoon, gentleman," he said. "How can I help you? Oh, it's Robert." He shook Robert's outstretched hand. "What brings you this way? Oh yes, and Oliver. Hello." Rachel's brother was wearing a bright red jacket. A real city man. "I'm afraid you're out of luck if you've come to see Rachel. She's away."

"Do you know where she's gone?" asked Bob. "When did she leave?"

Oliver looked disbelieving. "She never said anything to me about going away."

"It looked unpremeditated. Not that I take much notice of her comings and goings but I did see a car drive up, oh about a week ago now. The driver wasn't someone I recognised. She got in with a case, one of those inflight cases on wheels, and they drove off. Oh and just before they left, she wound down her window and let me have her house and car keys – handed them to me in an envelope and asked me to keep an eye on things."

"Who was the driver?"

"I don't know, I'm afraid. It wasn't anyone I know or have seen around the place."

That went well, Nicolas thought with relief, as Bob and Oliver got into their cars to leave. He held the gate open for them and closed it after them, watching the two cars bounce down the track, across the field, towards the further gate and the lane.

He continued to watch as one of the men – the one in the bright red jacket – held the gate open and bent to say something to the driver of the second car. Whatever it was he was saying went on for some time, which was worrying. Then both cars were gone and Nicolas was able to breathe freely again. He'd expected Oliver to ask for the keys in order to look around the house for clues as to Rachel's whereabouts. He was fairly confident that all looked normal, but you can never be sure you haven't overlooked a detail. He was glad he hadn't been tested to that extent.

He hurried inside to get the women's meal ready. He was very behindhand today, what with the trip to Exeter, the shopping fiasco, topped off with the visit of the two inquisitive men. It was all a strain. He didn't think he could continue like this for much longer. A solution would have to be found. Then he could go away on an extended trip abroad, and relax in the sun somewhere quiet.

Sally ran her spoon across the top of her frothy, creamy, sweet, hot chocolate. She added a generous splash of rum from her silver flask, then savoured the first taste of her favourite Swiss morning treat. Beyond the balcony of the hostel, fresh snow lay three foot deep on the wooden buildings of the resort and on the slopes above. The sky was utterly blue, the air crisply chill, the sun warm. She felt a smile spreading slowly across her face as she spotted Manoli climbing the short flight of steps to the balcony. Once again, the gorgeous Cypriot had turned up at the same time as she had. Life was good.

Angela watched Rachel nervously. She'd totally lost her cool. She was stamping between the two cells, in an absolute panic just because she couldn't find the sharp stone.

"What the fucking hell have you done with it?"

"Me? I haven't done anything with it."

"You had it last."

"I didn't. You did."

"*You* did! You marked the wall yesterday."

"I didn't. You've always been the one to mark the wall."

"No! You've taken a turn."

"I certainly haven't. And if I had, I'd have put the stone back in the place I've always kept it."

"Well, if that's so, where is it now? It's NOT THERE."

"That's because I haven't used it!"

Rachel must have heard this because she paused briefly before continuing her tirade.

"How the fucking hell can something go missing in this tiny space? It's driving me wild."

"I can see that. Come and sit down. You can have the chair. Try and keep calm. If you get in a state, you use up more oxygen. Then it's worse. It becomes a vicious downward spiral." She'd long ago learnt the truth of that.

Rachel continued to storm, chucking aside the duvet, the blanket, the thin pillows, lifting up the camping gaz, looking in the saucepan, scouring the walls for any ledges that might hold the stone … back and forth between the two chambers, energetically shouting and swearing.

Angela made herself as small as possible, sitting hunched and cross-legged on the bed in the inner chamber. She screwed up her eyes and buried her head in her arms, making a determined effort to regulate her own breathing. She must remain unaffected by Rachel's panic. It was stupid of Rachel to want to mark the days. She'd never bothered with such a fruitless exercise. The row of scratches that Rachel had made only accentuated the appalling passage of time. She muttered something to this effect.

"What did you say? *What the hell did you say?*"

"Nothing."

"Nothing? Of course you said nothing. You never say anything worth saying. It's no wonder Nicolas wanted to get rid of you."

Now Angela did raise her head and open her eyes. She regarded Rachel with utter astonishment. Rachel returned her look, with equal astonishment. There was a moment's silence in the cell. Then Rachel fell on the bed beside Angela, and wrapped her in her arms.

"Oh I didn't mean – I don't know what made me say – I don't know what got into me. Please forgive me. I didn't mean - I'm so sorry. You've been here for years, you've kept your – whatever it is you have – your calm, your sense. I've gone to pieces! And only after a few days! Oh, I'm useless." Rachel rocked herself to and fro as she repeated herself. "I'm so sorry, I didn't mean what I said."

Angela stroked Rachel's hair as she ranted on. Every so often she murmured something which she hoped would be soothing, but Rachel was entirely in the world of her own creation.

"It's that bloody flint stone. If it hadn't gone missing, I'd be able to mark the days. We definitely missed yesterday and the day before. I don't think I've made a mark for ages!"

"Well, never mind about that. It makes no difference if we know how many days you've been here or we don't."

"It *does* make a difference!"

"I don't see how. Time hasn't any meaning here."

"Oh but that's a dreadful attitude!"

"If the light didn't come on and off we wouldn't know if it was day or night."

"And we'd go mad!"

"Perhaps we've gone mad already!" Angela's smile was calm.

"I haven't gone mad." Rachel was indignant. "Neither have you," she added.

"I'm not so sure." Angela thought she'd been mad to let

Rachel persuade Nicolas to bring scissors, cooking gas, and matches to them. There was no knowing where that would lead. The idea came to her suddenly that Nicolas might be wanting Rachel to take some kind of disastrous action so that he would be justified in carrying out a final solution to his predicament. She knew him well enough. If a course of action suited him, he'd follow it, no matter its implications for others or even himself. She knew how the presence of Rachel had upset his routine, throwing him off balance; that is, if he'd any shred of balance to start with. Fortunately, for herself, she felt resigned to whatever lay ahead. No action was required of her. She wasn't afraid of death any longer. Living was something she did without having to do anything in particular. Her days slipped past, marked or unmarked. Perhaps she *was* mad to be so accepting. "Who's to say who's mad and who isn't?" she said aloud. "Perhaps I'm like that nun you're going to write about. She chose to live here for years and years."

"Ha. Yes. You must be like Elfrida. You've kept your faith. You pray to a divine being. It must help."

Lucy rang Sally. "If you can spare the time, I think it would be good if you came down for the weekend."

"I'm in Switzerland. I won't be home until Sunday. Has there been a development?"

"Yes. Bob and Oliver met at Priory Cottage. They saw Nicolas. No sign of Rachel. They are a bit uneasy. Nicolas said that a man had turned up in a car and driven Rachel away. She had a flight bag with her."

Sally could not respond at once. This was not right. Rachel wouldn't go away without telling her. Nor would she get involved with another man, without Sally knowing anything about it.

Lucy waited a second or two for Sally to speak before continuing. "You're uneasy too?"

"Yes. Certainly I am." Her mind was now working fast. Something bad had happened to Rachel. Nicolas's first wife had disappeared. She knew what she had to do. "I'll change my flight. Could Bob meet me at the station?"

Lucy felt a jolt of surprise. "Bob? I can ask him," she replied doubtfully. Perhaps Sally thought, as Rachel had thought, that she and Robert were husband and wife. "You do know Rob and I are just next door neighbours. My husband's called Tom and he's away a lot. There's nothing between Robert and me. We're just good friends and he does help me sometimes, so I can certainly ask him to meet you."

"Oh!" Sally realised her mistaken assumption. And Rachel's. "We thought, we both thought, Rachel thinks ..." She stopped, feeling foolish.

Lucy smiled at the way the two Londoners had jumped to the wrong conclusion. Her guess was right. It was a satisfactory explanation as to why both Rachel and Robert were on edge with each other. There was a strong attraction between them. Rachel had held back. Robert thought she disliked him. This could be put right – when she was found. At this, she remembered Angela's disappearance and felt a shiver of foreboding,

"But why not phone Robert yourself?" suggested Lucy. If Sally went to the cottage, it would be sensible if Robert was with her.

"I will." Yes, she'd ring Robert right away. They'd look for Rachel together. He didn't belong to anyone! He was a single man!

A FEW DAYS LATER

Nicolas was shaken by the incident in Exeter. He had never before walked out of a shop without paying. It was extremely upsetting the way he'd been accused of shop lifting. The shop assistant who'd follow him out didn't seem to believe it was a simple lapse of memory. Her attitude made him feel hot and angry. Oliver and Robert's visit had unnerved him as well. He resorted more frequently to the bottle of whisky, to soothe his nerves.

Most mornings, he woke up with a headache and the hollow feeling that he had committed some misdemeanour. What exactly it was, he couldn't at first remember. It was not shoplifting. That incident had been caused simply by a brief lack of concentration. There was something else that bothered him. Perhaps it was simply the burden of looking after two women.

It was the next Saturday that he woke to realise that he actually had forgotten something important. He'd forgotten to visit the cell the day before.

He reassured himself that this wasn't serious. Missing a meal wasn't the end of the world for Angela and Rachel. He could take them double rations today. While he prepared his regular breakfast - porridge, boiled egg and toast - he reviewed the situation. It was clear to him that the care of two women was telling on him. It had been viable when it was just Angela. With Rachel added, it was too much.

Yet he could not visualise getting rid of Rachel. Ever since she'd moved in next door, the glimpses he'd had of her long legs had given him exquisite pleasure. The sensation dated from the time when she'd leant over to reach something from the back seat of her Nissan just as he came out of his front gate. She was wearing very short, white shorts which were tightly stretched across a neat little bum. He liked to recall the sight, and its effect – still palpable in memory. He had been looking forward to the summer when she would want to wear shorts again, rather than hunch herself up under the duvet against the cave's dank cold. If it was a case of keeping only one of the two women, then it would be Rachel he would keep.

But how could this possibly work? Rachel would be missed, in a way that Angela hadn't been. She'd be reported missing. The police would call around.

She would have to disappear. They'd both have to disappear.

It must be painless.

He tapped his boiled egg and lifted its top open with a teaspoon, releasing the evocative smell of sulphur. Immediately the solution came to him. Exhaust fumes! In the past he'd read about a family slowly dying from carbon monoxide poisoning. Their gas boiler had needed cleaning. They'd been inhaling fumes which had slowly affected them, making them increasingly sleepy and indolent over a number of days. They failed to realise what was happening,

Later that morning, he drove the sit-on mower down to the workshop, a large coil of hose in its truck. He determined to set up the operation without delay. He'd fit one end of the hose onto the exhaust of the mower and the other end into the hose that emerged through the grille. Best not to delay but start at once before he thought better of it. He'd run the motor for half an hour at a time, over the next few days. It would be a humane death, a gentle falling asleep. He'd miss Angela – he'd miss them both, of course he would, but what else was he to do?

"Angela, do you know what I think? Nicolas will forget us again today, *on purpose*. I think he intends to starve us. We've got to take matters into our own hands."

Angela thought that would be a marvellous thing to do, but absolutely impossible. "How will we do that?"

"I have a plan."

"Oh yes?" Rachel's first plan had been to be extremely polite and helpful to Nicolas, winning him over – she assumed – into letting them both go. This was an exaggerated version of her own long-term strategy and it only served to prolong her powerlessness. The way Rachel thought she knew how to deal with Nicolas better than she did herself was becoming irritating. On the other hand it was a comfort to have someone else enduring the same existence. "Tell me what you're thinking."

"Scissors and stone," said Rachel.

"Yes?" Angela felt foreboding.

"Yes. We'll have to be strong and determined."

"What have you in mind?"

"An attack."

Rachel described what she visualised. They would stand either side of the door into the inner cell. Angela would be standing to the right of the opening, holding the stone. When Nicolas entered, she'd bury the stone in one of his eyes, the one nearest to her, and press it in as firmly as she could. She might not blind him permanently, but she'd injure his eye badly enough to blind him temporarily. Meanwhile, Rachel would plunge the scissors into his jugular vein from her position behind the door. They'd take him totally by surprise. They'd grab the chain of keys, unlock the outer door and escape before he knew what was happening,

"You think?" said Angela. "I can't imagine that working, for a single minute."

"Don't be so pessimistic. It's worth a try."

"Nothing's worth a try. We'll be worse off. You have no idea what Nicolas is capable of, when he loses his temper."

"What's the worst he can do? Okay, so he might kill us. But I'd rather go down fighting than just acquiesce to anything and everything he wants to do with us."

Rachel spent an hour slowly working on Angela. Eventually she persuaded her that it was the only solution. They could not bank on one of Rachel's friends noticing her absence and doing something about it. "I have very few real friends," she told Angela. "No-one round here will notice I'm missing for ages. I am not going to wait for a rescue that may not ever happen."

Angela relapsed into silence. She could not convince Rachel not to attack Nicolas. Although she knew it was a terrible mistake to try something that would fail, the easiest course was to go along with it. Whatever was going to happen was going to happen, whatever she did or didn't do.

Nicolas drove the sit-on mower down to the workshop, the long hose and the basket of food in its grass-catcher trailer. After parking and switching off the engine, he set up the hose, forcing one end onto the exhaust pipe and the other through the grille. He'd take the food to the women before putting his plan into action.

What a rigmarole it was. And what complications arise once you relax rules. He should never have let the women have the run of both chambers. Nowadays, he had to get them into the inner cell before he could bring stuff into the outer chamber. Then the container of water, the basket of food and the clean loo bucket had to be brought into the first chamber before locking the outer door behind him and opening the inner door to change the loo bucket. At least, Rachel was always grateful. The way she looked up and smiled at him was a pleasure. He might decide not to run the engine. After all, warmer weather and shorts-wearing would be here before too long.

As he unlocked and then opened the first door, he felt a piercing pain in one eye, swiftly followed by a sharp blow to his neck. He whirled around, understanding that he'd been attacked. The women had gone for him. It was beyond belief! He struck out wildly, hitting at whatever he could, despite blood blinding him and gushing down his neck. This was monstrous! Angela's hand was pressed against his face, his eye, something was on his neck, stinging sharply like a wasp. He flung the basket at Angela and she dropped her hand; a stone fell to the floor; he swung round and grabbed Rachel's arm. She was holding to his neck something that glinted. He forced her hand away. The scissors! The treacherous bitch! He knew he should never trust women.

With all the strength he could muster despite his pain, he pushed the women backwards into the cell and locked the door on them. He staggered out, holding his handkerchief to his face. Blood throbbed somewhere in the side of his neck. He would need to get to the first aid kit but first he'd set the engine running. He'd run it for a little while each day until he was certain it had done its job. He wouldn't go back into the cell. He wouldn't risk another attack by the mad women. He'd listen at the grille.

Until there was no sound.

Robert parked his pick-up in the 20 minute zone outside Exeter St David's station. He doubted that Sally knew the colour or make of his vehicle, so he kept his attention on the people emerging at the exit. He was sure he would recognise Sally. A lot of black hair, not tall and not exactly fat, but with a well-rounded figure and pink cheeks to match. When he did spot her, it was the disturbance in her path that made her stand out. She came in a whirl of bags, her open coat flapping, shedding newspapers and magazines, spilling apples, laughing her apologies to the people in her wake.

"Robert!" She was a good twenty feet away, waving a bag vigorously at him.

He greeted her with a smile of pleasure. Yes, this was the Sally he recognised, who enthused about his work and tried to influence Rachel's choices. No hope of that – Rachel was unswayable in her views. That was admirable, unless her view was founded on a misapprehension. Now that he understood her reason for steering clear of him - at least, he hoped there wasn't a deeper reason – then he was intent on seeing her and getting her mind straight on his neighbourly friendship with Lucy. He was single. So was she!

He got out of the car. Sally was at his side. "Have you been waiting AGES?"

They spent the drive to Priory Cottage conferring about Rachel. They'd both come to the conclusion that her unannounced and inexplicable absence was a cause for great concern. Nicolas's wife had disappeared, too. It was a relief for both of them that they could share their anxiety.

"Do you know what I think?" said Sally. "I think she went exploring the ruins and Nicolas caught her."

Robert had repeatedly thought of that, too. It filled him with dread.

"She may have tried to find Elfrida's cell. I'm going to confront him."

"Sally, are you sure? What if Nicolas really has - done something – I mean, we can't be sure about anything – and we know he's strange. I don't think you should stay alone in the cottage. Come back with me. Lucy can put you up."

"Oh, I can manage Nicolas, whatever he tries on."

Robert didn't think it wise to be so upbeat. He made up his mind that he'd stick around, all night if necessary. "Let's both confront Nicolas," he said as they turned in by the Torridon sign.

Sally got out to open the gate. "I hope he's here. I'd like to get this over."

Nicolas was in the downstairs cloakroom bathing the blood from his face when he heard a car's wheels in the gravel of the parking space. "God damn and blast it!" he exclaimed aloud. He crouched down out of sight of the mirror as though that would make him invisible to whoever had turned up. He listened intently.

After some minutes, there was a knock on the front door.

"Nicolas? Hello? Are you there?"

He recognised Robert's voice. He dried his face and went to open the front door, composing his features as he did so.

"Oh good morning, Bob." He was relieved to hear himself sounding normally urbane, although on a register higher than usual. "What brings you here again so soon? With Sally, I see." He noted their expressions. Perhaps he hadn't removed all the blood.

Their voices mingled. "We just need to check the cottage. See everything's all right. On Rachel's behalf. Can we have her keys, please? Nicolas? You okay? You do have her keys, don't you? You said when I was here with her brother…."

It was one of those moments that seem to last for ever, as though time itself had stopped. Nicolas was transfixed, held in the gaze of Robert and Sally. They were waiting for something from him, but he couldn't work out what he could do or say. All his explanations, and all his problems, tumbled one after the other through his mind, but his brain was frozen.

The crunch had come, he realised. He'd been jumped into a rapid decision. No time for bottles of whisky, no time for poison, no time for fumes, he must act. But how?

Behind the two on his doorstep, through the evergreen archway to the parking space, he could see Rachel's blue Nissan. Into his foggy brain came the image of Rachel in her little white shorts. It swept all other thoughts from his mind, save one. He could not extinguish that glowing life. The solution came to him, like the appearance of the full moon through clouds. It was as though he'd always known what he could and would do in the end.

Shutting the door on Robert and Sally, he worked fast, collecting a few clothes, his stock of cash, his passport. Then out of the back door, down the garden, to his workshop and around the back to the far side of the cell's hillock. He yanked the hose out of the grille near the top. Then he hurried around the hill to leave all his keys, those of Torridon, Priory Cottage and the keys to Elfrida's cell, all together in a heap on the grass by the entrance. He would have liked to say good-bye. It seemed to him bad form to leave without any kind of farewell. But there was no time to lose. He had to get away fast before Sally and Robert began investigating. Perhaps he had an hour's start? He'd entertained this plan in a vague way several times, always preferring it to a violent solution. It was just a matter of putting it into action: the drive to Plymouth, the overnight ferry to St Malo, then off south...

But now back to the house fast. to pick up his bag, run through the kitchen, out of the back door, across the stable yard, past the stables – casting a swift, regretful glance at the ceiling-high stacks of paintings, furniture, boxes - to the barn; then into the Navara, hurling his bag onto the back seat, out of the barn and straight onto the track, no bother of a gate at this point, what a benefit. In the driving mirror he caught a glimpse of Bob and Sally standing together by his front gate, framed by the leylandii hedge, gazing after him. He could imagine their expressions and heard his own gleeful bark of triumph. Sometimes Toad of The Wind in the Willows came to mind. A fellow spirit! He was going to deserve the holiday that would last the rest of his life.

SIX MONTHS LATER

Rachel and Robert had taken a rug into the garden to lie in the shade of an apple tree. Their murmured conversation came and went as they drifted in and out of sleep. Rachel said she had never been happier. Robert said the same. And so did Angela next door.

Angela was going to come over for a meal that evening, as she usually did on a Saturday, her busiest day. The priory, open from 10 a.m. to 6 p.m, had become a popular place to visit, its attraction lying not so much in the medieval ruins as in Elfrida's cell, made famous by its recent occupants. Rachel was unsettled by the visitors' morbid fascination in a place that had been the setting of such a nightmare. She guessed that if she and Angela were still there, visitors would arrive in even greater numbers. She imagined looking up at a horde of faces peering in at them through the grille: wild animals in a cage. She and Robert had only agreed that Angela could go ahead with her ideas, so long as the public weren't allowed near Torridon and Priory Cottage. The public parked their cars in the Middletons' field which had a freshly-made entrance through the hedge, giving immediate access to the priory ruins. The Middletons were happy with the new source of income from the parking fees and the cream teas that Betty laid on in the farmhouse.

So, thankfully, all this new activity went on at a distance from her new life with Robert in Priory Cottage. She could mostly forget about the crowds and – sometimes - her ordeal. Unlike Angela, who was creating a business from her experience and thriving on the interest in her story. It was as though she was at last making sense of her life. She seemed undamaged by her long imprisonment. "After all," she told them, "it was really no different from my life with Nicolas above ground. And in some ways better."

"Staggering," said Robert.

Rachel, lying on the rug, nestled her head in the hollow of his shoulder. A thrush was singing nearby. My life could not be better, she thought. Her mind drifted to the pages she had so far created for Elfrida's story. She was pleased with the way she was achieving, with acrylic paints, the glowing colours of an illuminated manuscript. She remembered her thoughts to lighten the story by introducing a Brother Henry who would somehow rescue Elfrida and turn her fate around, from dark to light. Lines came to her haltingly. Perhaps she would not write the story at all but use as text the verse written originally by the builder of Torridon: the Reverend Eliot McGelligott. She remembered the name well, it was as *dum de dum* as the verse he'd written. *Elfrida was a maid so pure* ... yes, she would write in fine italics two verses on each page, and it would end with Brother Henry.

"Rachel! Rachel?"

Robert woke her with a mug of tea.

"Listen to this," she told him. "I think I've got the right ending.

"*As sweetly sings the nightingale*
So Elfrida's soul sang psalms
While through long nights of love she lay
In Brother Henry's arms."

Robert lay down beside her, rearranging his arm once more so she could nestle her head on his shoulder. "Am I Brother Henry?" he asked.

"In a way."

There's a resort on the Black Sea, near the border between Bulgaria and Rumania, which suits Nicolas well, just for the time being. He is going back and forth between the two countries dealing in gold. He always knew that his grandfather's hoard of pocket watches, bracelets, medallions, rings, many of them in 18 carat gold, would be a lifeline. He'd always kept them in a hidden layer of his suitcase, against a sudden unpremeditated departure from Torridon. Did he always know this would happen? No, you can't ever know what will happen. The secret is to remain flexible, to have fast responses, to be ready for anything. When he was a schoolboy, he was a good fielder. His hand would shoot out and catch the cricket ball, against all odds, to great applause.

Today he's sitting on the veranda of a bar, built out over the shingle beach. The light on the sea is silver. An ash-grey haze obscures the sun.

"No swim today, Mister Eliot?"

"No swim."

"Maybe tomorrow?"

"Maybe."

No plans. Play it by ear. A wave of sadness sweeps through him. He thinks of Angela. It had been marvellous for so long. A steady routine. He'd known exactly what he had to do, regularly every day, a daily task, and there she was, every day, meekly waiting for him. Until that bloody Rachel woman had come along.

Rachel, with her long legs emerging from her tiny white shorts.

He sighed. He'd done the right thing. He'd been chivalrous.

"Another whisky, Mister Eliot?"

He nodded.

Another whisky Mister Eliot will continue for how long? He's not exactly impatient but he is looking forward to the day when there'll be another sort of voice at his shoulder, heralding a long journey back to England under escort. He's ready for anything. It has been worth it. And Angela will visit him. He's sure of that. His Angel.

THE END

ABOUT THE AUTHOR

Susan Barrett

Susan's first novel was published by Michael Joseph in 1969. Film rights were sold. Susan went on to have six more novels published by Michael Joseph, Hamish Hamilton and Collins, in hardback and paperback, in UK and US. A television play she wrote called The Portrait was produced by LWT and starred Annette Crosbie and Maurice Denham. She has written a number of children's books illustrated by her artist husband Peter Barrett. They have worked together on two books with Greece as subject matter, having spent many years in that country. Latterly, Susan converted her early, traditionally published novels into ebook editions for Kindle, as well as producing her recent non-fiction and fiction titles on KDP as paperbacks and ebooks. Susan and Peter Barrett live in Devon, the county where Susan was born and brought up. Their son lives in New Zealand, and their daughter in their nearest village. They are now great grandparents and are still working away in studio and study.

PRAISE FOR AUTHOR

Jam Today
"A jolly romp, I found this hilarious."

- DAILY TELEGRAPH

Moses
"One of the wittiest novels I've read recently."

- DEREK STANFORD, THE SCOTSMAN

Noah's Ark
"A delightful comedy of manners, astringent enough not to be coy and thoughtful enough not to be frivolous."

- FRANCIS KING, SUNDAY TELEGRAPH

Private View
"Highly professional and enjoyable."

- TIMES LITERARY SUPPLEMENT

Rubbish
"Taking a few swipes at materialistic society on her way, Mrs Barrett contrives some marvellous muddles."

- SUNDAY TELEGRAPH

The Beacon
"What lifts The Beacon onto a different plane is Susan Barrett's understanding of people."

- MARTYN GOFF, DAILY TELEGRAPH

Stephen and Violet
"A psychological itinerary, movingly traced with great insight and skill."

- PATRICK LEIGH FERMOR

Greek Gold
"I have some knowledge, but not as much as hers, when it comes to the dark, brave days of the war and after, and she never hits a wrong note. An exciting and moving piece of work. F.R."

- FREDERICK RAPHAEL

A Home from Home
"I enjoyed A Home from Home, and admired Susan Barrett's im-

aginative verve and technical skill. The idiosyncratic setting of the care home is very convincing, and sheer multiplicity of the well-characterised staff and inmates is impressive. So are their complex interrelationships and their often surprising and far-reaching backgrounds. She brings off one of the best things that a novelist can do – the creation of a world – and writes about it both vividly and elegantly.'

- MICHAEL FRAYN

Travels with a Wildlife Artist, with Peter Barrett
"Nothing escapes the author's eye ...The sort of book you wish you had written yourself."

- GERALD DURRELLL

BOOKS BY THIS AUTHOR

Greek Gold

This is the story of a wartime hero and the daughter he never knew. In 1943, Alex, a newly married SOE agent, is dropped into German-occupied northern Greece. Badly hurt on landing, separated from supplies and his wireless operator, he gets in with the 'wrong' band of resistance fighters. His second mistake is to fall in love with a Rumanian-Greek, Ileana. Within a couple of months, he is dead. His daughter Helen, born after he was killed and now a widow herself, visits the scene of his death, hoping to find out more about his heroic action. Slowly she learns the truth from the villagers, in the company of newly-met Heinrich, a German plant collector, lecturer and widower. Helen revises the picture of her father. He was not the hero she thought he was but his all-too-human failings have brought him alive for her, with memories to cherish.

A Home From Home

Malpractice and mayhem - the events of a single day at a care home are described with humour and compassion in this fast-paced novel. Edith was a child when Stoneycrest was her family home. Now she's an alert and watchful resident. She hatches a plot to expose the malpractice she sees going on around her, aided and abetted by Len, another resident. Spiro, the owner, has his own plans for Stoneycrest, as does his love on the side, Marion the matron of the home. Tass, his niece, is more straightforward in her aims. She just wants lots of cash from Spiro. The day unfolds in surprising ways, as the characters pursue their own ends with varying degrees of calamity and success. 'A Home from Home' is a novel which brings together once again the particular blend of humour and compassion for which this long-established writer is known. Thought-provoking entertainment is Susan Barrett's stock in trade.

White Lies

.White Lies a poignant tale which explores the joys and hazards of adoption, skilfully and movingly told from the perspectives of three women over half a century. Beth is a guest at a wedding. The bride is Tess, her natural daughter, who'd been adopted as a baby. During the moments leading up to the marriage ceremony, Beth remembers the lifetime events that have led to her present state of sick fear. Recent revelations have made her suspect that the bridegroom is the first child she'd given up for adoption, and therefore Tess's half-brother. Will she speak of this impediment to matrimony, as invited by the priest, or forever hold her peace? White Lies gives the answer in a way that reveals the complexities of truth-telling in the context of parenthood and adoption. The reader's sympathy is engaged with each woman in turn, as the intricacies of the plot demonstrate how nature and nurture interplay in the formation of personality. Susan Barrett is an experienced writer of fact and fiction published by traditional publishers in hardback and paperback in UK and USA. She has also produced Kindle editions of her previously published novels, and self-published recent work.

Alive In World War Two

Alive in World War Two weaves together extracts from wartime newsletters exchanged between the members of a scattered family with the author's own memories of a wartime childhood in Devon, within the context of events in the world today.

The cousins were typical of the generation who responded to Churchill's eloquence when Britain defied Hitler: they were ordinary people, unknown, unhonoured and remarkable only for their resilience. Today, we are in the midst of a different kind o war, with no end in sight. The present commentary and memoir is a salute to the cousins of the Chronicle for the way they did their best in their time and place, and an invocation of their spirit. On the scale of human evolution, wherever and whenever we live, we are all cousins working out how best to live our lives in the conditions of our own times.

The Garden Of The Grandfather, Life In Greece In The 1960S

When Peter and Susan Barrett met and married in 1960, they shared similar ambitions – Peter to paint for a living, and Susan to write novels. This, their latest book together, is a homage to Greece, the country which provided the context and stimuli at the start of their careers and continues to do so. Black and white photographs taken at the time, combined with sketches and text. capture a simpler way of life that has generally disappeared. By describing their personal experience at a particular period in a particular country, their memoir reflects universal themes in a changing world.
It is their second book with Greece as subject matter. This is the ebook edition. It's also available as a softback from the authors' own website, susanbarrettwriter.com

Travels With A Wildlife Artist, The Living Landscape Of Greece

Published in 1986 and still available second hand, this is the Barretts' first book on Greece, its places and its people. In text and pictures, they describe what they saw when travelling around the country, by road and sea, in the 1980s.

'A book you wish you had written yourself,' Gerald Durrell.

AND MORE

Have a look at my website
https://susanbarrettwriter.com

Printed in Poland
by Amazon Fulfillment
Poland Sp. z o.o., Wrocław